Maisie Raine was a history teacher in a North East Comprehensive School. When she left teaching, she had time to fulfil her ambition, and began writing for children. She is passionate about history and folklore and would like to encourage young people to be curious about the world around them, and to question everything they see. Abi and her friends from Dunchester were first introduced in the book "Summer of the Witch."

Maisie lives in rural County Durham, on a dairy farm on top of a hill with partner Barry and a dog called Alfie. Her home overlooks a beautiful valley and a village surprisingly similar to "Dunchester"!

AUTUMN FOR A MAGUS

Maisie Raine

AUTUMN FOR A MAGUS

A CIP catalogue record for this title is
available from the British Library.

ISBN: 978-0-9576492-0-0

This is a work of fiction.
Names, characters, places and incidents originate from the
writer's imagination. Any resemblance to actual persons,
living or dead, is purely coincidental.

First published in 2013.

BRAVE ARTHUR THE KING...

The dragon may prowl in the streets of the city,
And the world may turn out to be not as it seems,
And many a job may be axed by tomorrow,
And we may be obliged to abandon our dreams.
"But bring in the fool in his motley and bells
And remember the minstrels who taught you to sing,
And the quest it begins with the steps of the dance, Won't
you please find your partners" said Arthur the King.

So we'll kindle a beacon on every high mountain
To the sound of our music the valleys shall ring
To waken the sleepers of long vanished ages
To welcome the knights and brave Arthur the King.

There are times when the fog is so thick on the hills,
Fell enchantments have settled on river and lake
And the poisons have sunk so far into the earth
That we ask "Is there anything left there to wake?"
"But bring in the morris, the sword dance and step dance
The music is there and you know how to sing.
For the quest it begins with a song from the heart.
Won't you join in the chorus," said Arthur the King.

So we'll kindle a beacon on every high mountain,
To the sound of our music the valleys shall ring
To waken the sleepers of long vanished ages,
To welcome the knights and brave Arthur the King.

AUTUMN FOR A MAGUS

Abi returns to Dunchester a year after her adventures there when she became aware of the mysterious powers present in the valley. The spirit of Jane Wake, a woman put to death for witchcraft centuries before, returned to the village, seeking revenge on her own people who had betrayed her. Abi and her friends brought peace to Jane at last.

On her return, she finds everyone talking about a millionaire, Zak Rivers, who has come to live in the area. He's a man of mystery, eager to discover the secrets of earth magic present in the valley, and to use them for his own ends. In an excavation on the ancient Maiden's Hill, Zak finds the preserved body of a hermit who lived 2,000 years ago and seeks to bring the man back to life. Zak plans to use the magical knowledge the man possesses to bring dark forces into the valley, gaining for himself enormous powers.

This will be a battle between good and evil, and the results could affect the future of our whole world. Abi and her group of friends must discover Zak's plan and work out how to stop it succeeding, but the ancient season of Samhain is fast approaching, a time when evil is at its most powerful...

DUNCHESTER

Dunchester village lies in a secluded County Durham valley. It's a quiet, sleepy place where nothing much seems to happen, but mysterious forces have existed in the valley since the beginning of time. Electrical and mechanical objects often won't work, and clocks seem to have a mind of their own. Many local people have stories to tell, and can recall strange happenings and ghostly visitations. You might hear some of these tales- if it's felt you can be trusted... Often, you may just catch a glimpse of a dark figure disappearing close by, or something just about to happen at the very second you look away.

Everyone has their theory about why weird things happen in Dunchester, -maybe the cause is electrical or magnetic force fields present in the valley, or perhaps there's a geological reason, with some weakness of the earth's crust existing in that spot, or a crack occurring deep underground. Could ley lines be responsible for the peculiar nature of the valley? Several of these ancient 'lines of power' run through the area and meet in Dunchester village. And who is the mysterious hunter who has appeared for centuries and acts as the guardian spirit of the site, protecting the valley and its inhabitants?

Whatever the secrets of the valley may be, the old 'uns keep their counsel and don't say much, they don't trust outsiders......

Chapter One

~~~~~

DUNCHESTER'S VERY OWN
MULTI MILLIONAIRE!

As the train slowed and squealed its way into Durham station, Abi stood up, reaching for her travel bag in the rack above her seat. She suddenly realised she'd been reading curled up in the same position for ages, and placing her hands in the small of her back she gratefully stretched her spine. She'd had a good journey, the countryside had been bathed in the mellow sunlight of early autumn, and she was now looking forward to reaching her destination in the north east corner of the country. Abi sank back into her seat so that she could fully enjoy this first sight of the city she loved.

And here was Durham again! She looked down on the toy-sized houses grouped together, higgledy piggledy, the tiny people hurrying along, intent upon their own business, and the hints of mysterious winding streets disappearing among the buildings then reappearing further on. The solid, massive cathedral and castle loomed over the scene, guardians of the city for centuries, and Abi remembered the legend describing the origins of Durham and its great church.

In the Tenth Century, the monks from Holy Island fled from the fierce Viking raiders from across the North Sea. They took with them the body of their beloved Saint Cuthbert, desperately seeking a place of safety for his earthly remains. The holy men wandered for a long time, before finally reaching the banks of the River Wear. Here, Cuthbert's body became so heavy that it was impossible for the monks to go any further. It seemed that the saint was telling them something. Then Cuthbert himself appeared to them, saying that he wished his body to rest in the place called Dunholme. The monks had no idea about where this site could be, but then they heard two women talking about a lost cow.

One woman told her friend she had last seen the cow

grazing on Dunholme- the Hill Island. The monks asked the women where this place was, and found that they could now move Cuthbert's body easily. They came at last to Dunholme, a peninsula formed by a curve in the River Wear. Here, they built a small chapel to house their holy relics, and over the centuries, the humble building had grown into a great and beautiful cathedral, famous across the world.

Abi loved this old story. "So all of this happened because of a lost cow hundreds of years ago!" she thought to herself. "The cathedral, the city, all the people who live here, and the thousands who come to visit-everything! Amazing!" She picked up her bag and made her way to the door as the train finally shuddered to a stop. Through the window she spotted Dad and her friend Kate among the crowd on the platform, and she waved at them excitedly. It had been just over a year since her first visit to the north east, and she'd kept in close touch with the friends she'd made then, Kate and her brothers Tom and Stuart. Now she was back to stay with her dad for a month or so while her mother was doing some training course in London. Abi had been enrolled into the local Comprehensive school with her friends, and she was looking forward to spending a lot of time with the people from Crow Hill Farm.

David hurried through the throng of people on the platform and reaching her, gave her a big hug, slinging her bag easily over his shoulder. Kate was next to hug her, then everyone was talking at the same time as they made their way to the station car park. How had the journey been? How was everyone at the farm? And Buster? And Alfie and the cats? News was exchanged and questions answered with more questions, no one really listening closely, but feeling happy to be together, and completely at ease with each other.

As she settled into the car for the drive to Dunchester, Abi remembered how shy and awkward she'd felt on her first visit to the valley. She'd learned a lot about herself at that time, and through her experiences and the friendships she'd made, she had developed confidence in herself. She'd also discovered a deep love of history, although this was a very personal thing and the periods and themes she researched owed little to the sometimes boring lessons of "Sell By" Selby, her teacher at school. Grandad Bill had taught her that history was so much more than names and dates belonging to the long-gone past, it was a vibrant, living thing, concerning real people, their lives and emotions and beliefs. Abi had also become fascinated by ideas of earth magic, the existence of ancient forces which affect the world around us. She kept that interest strictly to herself. How weird would her friends in class think that was!

"So what's new in Dunchester?" Abi asked Kate during a lull in the conversation.

"Not much" Kate, sitting in the back seat of the car made a face. "Nothing much ever happens in Dunchester." She stopped abruptly, remembering last summer, when she and the others had become involved in the story of the witch woman, Jane Wake. That had been a scary time, and many mysterious things had certainly happened then!

"There's our new multi millionaire" David reminded her.

"That's a big bit of news for the village!"

"Yeah-you told me about him,-Zak something or other, and he's bought Derwent Hall" Abi broke in. "And you said he's excavating on Maiden Hill. I was surprised that your grandfather would let him do something like that, feeling as he does about keeping the land safe."

"He's called Zak Rivers, and Grandad did take a lot of persuasion before he let him start to dig, but Zak had done tons of research about the hill. You know that Grandad always had ideas of his own about its importance in the past, so when Zak came up with plans for a dig at his own expense, he couldn't resist it. He's laid down loads of rules for Zak, mind. The work can only go on for a certain time, and when it's all over, Zak must make sure that the hill is returned to exactly the way it was. Anyway, I think Zak set out to charm Grandad, like he does with a lot of other people in the valley. He seems to get his way in most things!"

"He's certainly spending a pile of money" David slowed the car's speed as they entered the village. "He's given work to lots of local people, doing the Hall up and sorting out the gardens and grounds, No one seems to know where his money comes from. There are all kinds of rumours about him, they say he's made a fortune doing business on the internet, but who knows? He's very careful when you talk to him, pleasant enough, but he doesn't give much away about himself. I just wonder why he's doing all this-what's in it for him? Mind, he did make an honest worker out of Jonty Ginks, even if it only lasted a couple of days!"

Abi thought about Derwent Hall as it had been last year, neglected and sad looking, a rambling stone building, much added to over the years and set among overgrown gardens and grounds. She had often imagined how the Hall could be made bright and cheerful again.

"This Zak must be really popular, buying that old place and bringing so much work and money into the village" she said thoughtfully.

"The village is divided about that, Abi" her Dad shook his head. "Some people think he's wonderful, the best thing to happen to Dunchester in years, but others are not at all happy. He wants to change things, you see, and the valley people don't like changes. And they're wondering what's in this for Mr. Rivers,-but I suppose we'll find that out in time."

The car had been climbing the steep hill from the village, and now they turned into the track leading to Crow hill Farm. They branched off along the drive to the cottage where David and Christine lived, through the avenue of dense bushes which almost met overhead. When they stopped, Kate slipped out of the car, and after arranging to meet Abi next morning, waved to Christine waiting at the front door and set off up the path to her home. As always the cats, brothers George and Henry were sitting with Christine, and Abi received yet another hug from her while David brought her bag from the car. Abi liked Christine and looked forward to hearing all the local gossip over supper.

She was pleased to find her room was exactly as she remembered it, and from the window, Abi looked out across the ancient valley, the village of Dunchester lying hidden within a fold of land. She'd last seen this view in high summer, during a hot, dry season when the spirit of Jane Wake had been woken and had vowed to punish the local folk she believed had betrayed her. Abi had felt a strange bond with the witch woman,-a connection which she could

20

still not understand. She had started to learn about the mysterious forces which dwelt within the earth, and within stones and trees. Magnetism, electrical power, faults deep in the earth's surface, or the influence of the many ley lines which were said to meet and intersect in the valley-she had heard all the theories which sought to explain the unaccountable happenings within this area. Whatever the answer may be, Abi knew for certain that the valley was a place of many mysteries.

She saw that late summer was slowly moving into autumn. Long evening shadows crept over the fields, and the earth felt calm and at rest, drawing breath after the labours of the growing and harvest times. Abi was glad to be back here, and she hurried to have a quick wash before Christine called her to come to supper.

The meal was really good, chicken cooked in a rich sauce of red peppers and onions and Abi discovered she was starving after her long journey. Christine chattered about the local people Abi knew, and told her a lot more about the excavations on Maiden Hill, now well into the time limit Bill Oaken had set for Zak Rivers. She obviously liked the newcomer, and enthused about his kindness and generosity, and his genuine passion for local history and folklore.

"You know, Grandad Bill has always believed the Hill was an important religious site long before written history" she said, passing David more vegetables. "In the old maps, its real name is Maiden's Dance, and Bill thinks sacred ceremonies would have taken place there. When Zak came along and said he wanted to pay for excavations, Bill couldn't refuse although he did set all kinds of conditions about what Zak could and couldn't do. The hill must be disturbed as little as possible."

Abi had a strong feeling that David had been less impressed with Zak Rivers, although he hadn't added to the conversation.

"So Old Bill likes this Zak?" she asked casually. Abi didn't know why she asked the question, but she felt it was important. A shadow passed over Christine's face.

"That's the strange thing, Abi. At first, they got on really well, they spent a lot of time together, and Zak asked him all

21

about the local people, and the history and legends of the valley. Zak had read about the area before moving here, and he badly wanted to fit in with the local community. Lately, though, since the dig began, Bill's changed towards Zak. Bill's not said much to me, but I get the feeling that he's become wary about him, and he's watching him. Zak hasn't been invited up to the farm in ages, and he was always up there, the two of them talking about all kinds of things and drinking their huge mugs of strong tea. Maybe Bill has got some odd idea stuck in his mind, older people often do for no good reason." Her voice tailed off, as if she had caught herself saying something disloyal about her friend.

"Anyway" she finished. "Let's hope Zak comes up with some really good finds, and he's able to fill in some of the missing history of the hill. That would please Old Bill, and it would be fantastic for the University. Zak's using some Durham archaeological students on the work, and he's promised to request that some of the finds are donated to my department."

Abi noticed that David had said nothing for a long time. Maybe he wasn't impressed by this millionaire stranger. She sipped her water and thought about what she had learned about Zak Rivers. Somehow, he seemed too good to be true, bringing all this money and work into the village and putting up a lot of his own cash to excavate Maiden Hill, that must be costing a fortune. What did he hope to gain from all this? And why come to Dunchester, of all places, this tiny dot on the map, unknown outside the region? Why had he taken the time and the effort to learn so much about the valley? There was something not right about all this, she decided. Things didn't fit together, a lot of questions needed answers. Abi thought about her friend Grandad Bill. She would trust his judgement about anything, and if he had doubts about Zak Rivers, there must be good reason. She would talk to him the first chance she got.

Chapter Two

~~~~~

ZAK RIVERS

Next morning was a beautiful late summer Saturday, bright, sunny and crisp. David had to go into work, and had left earlier, and Christine had also made an early start, preparing piles of sandwiches to take to her friends working up at the dig. Chatting to her as she buttered bread, Abi prepared tea and cereal for herself, then they were interrupted by a tap on the glass pane of the kitchen door-Tom, Stuart and Kate had arrived, escorted by their dog, Alfie. The big dog recognised Abi immediately and led the way inside to greet her, his shaggy tail waving like a flag.

Then came more hugs (my friends are very huggy people!) Abi thought,-and back slaps from the boys, accompanied by wet kisses from Alfie. Tom decided he wouldn't mind trying some of the sandwiches, and at Christine's suggestion, Kate turned on the kettle to make tea for everyone. Tom and Stuart began telling Abi funny and frightening stories about the teachers she'd meet on Monday morning, and Kate, more practical, had printed her a copy of her timetable and brought her the books she'd need for her first lessons. The girls were to be in the same tutor group, and Kate quickly told her about her form tutor and some of the kids in the group. Abi felt excited and nervous about meeting all these new people, and she was glad that Kate would be with her.

Christine set off with the sandwiches, flasks of coffee and bottles of water, telling them they would be very welcome if they wanted to come and see what was happening at the site. The friends decided to walk into Dunchester, and Alfie, who had hoped to be going with them, was very indignant when he was left at the farm. They left him staring after them before turning his back in disgust.

"Just look at that" laughed Stuart. "He's in a big huff with us now!

23

The village was just as Abi remembered it, except for a smart Italian restaurant which had opened in the High Street. Busy shoppers went about their tasks, and Tom suddenly realised he was starving and badly needed a coke and a sausage roll before they went any further. Kate eyed him coldly. She despaired of her brother and his ever lasting hunger, especially as he never put on extra weight.

They spent a pleasant hour in the small coffee shop, catching up on their individual bits of news. Abi looked at the rest of the group, talking and laughing around their favourite table set in the window bay and overlooking the busy main street of the village. It felt good to be back here with her friends, looking just the same as they were a year ago, and yet she thought she could notice tiny changes in their faces, so slight that they couldn't be described.

"We're all getting older!" she thought, feeling a little bit sad. "We're all growing up, that's what it is!"

They explored the shops in the village and Abi visited the statue of Jane Wake, set up on the green by Grandad Bill. She thought it looked beautiful, simple and moving. The young woman was portrayed with open arms stretched wide, in a gesture of love and hope. Now Jane and her true story would never be forgotten by her own people.

They decided to visit the excavations on Maiden Hill. Abi was really looking forward to experiencing her first taste of archaeology and the others, although they had seen the site several times, were still excited about what might be found inside the hill they had played on and always thought of as their own. The friends set off, crossing the car park behind the shops. There was a large black people carrier parked in a space away from any other vehicle. Three men dressed in jeans and tee shirts were loading several carrier bags into the back of the motor, and Abi guessed that this had been a weekend food shopping trip.

The men completed their task, and one of them appeared to be giving instructions as he opened the driver's door. Somehow, Abi knew that this slight, shaven headed man was the mysterious Zak Rivers. She was certain she had made no sound, but as if he had heard his name called out loud, the man lifted his head and turned towards her, taking off the dark glasses he was wearing. Zak Rivers smiled. His smile was chilling, not touching his eyes which stared unblinking into hers, causing her to feel suddenly cold and making her look away. The sun went behind a cloud and the people carrier slowly moved off.

As Abi dropped her eyes from the cold stare, she noticed that the others had also avoided looking at the three men, although she sensed that if she'd asked them the reason, they could give no answer. They took the path up to Maiden Hill in silence, not talking or laughing, as if they had all been affected by the meeting in the car park.

On the hill, they found the students taking a break with the drinks and sandwiches Christine had brought for them. Abi had imagined that archaeology students would be very serious people, the boys wearing beards and checked woollen shirts, and the girls in thick glasses with their hair pulled back in tight buns. She was mistaken-all of them wore jeans and university sweat shirts, and their conversation was about local football teams and some party they were all going to that night. They treated their tutor, Rob Dent, with endless jokes about his age and being "past it" but Abi noticed that they still listened with a lot of respect to whatever he said. They all shared drinks, and Tom declared that he'd love a sandwich, if there was one going spare. Kate raised her eyes in disgust, but Tom ignored the look and gladly helped himself to a bun filled with ham.

All of the students were aware that the time they had been granted was growing short, and even though the results of their search had so far been disappointing, there was still a feeling of quiet confidence among the group, as if hopes were still high that their hard work would be rewarded soon.

"We think we might have found traces of a stone circle, which should please your grandad, he always insisted there had to be one" Rob told the friends. "And there's something interesting coming up on the heat imaging equipment to suggest that there may be some kind of cave behind that lot" he nodded towards the face of the hill, where the lower levels of soil were slowly being exposed. "Could be that fits in with the old stories that a hermit lived here at one time. We may have some big surprises yet!"

"So when was the hermit supposed to live here?" Kate asked, dropping her empty water bottle into a nearby rubbish bucket. "How long ago would that be?"

Rob shrugged and puffed out his cheeks in thought. "I should think we're looking at the very early Christian period, at the time the Romans were leaving Britain, so anything we do find might be very interesting!"

Stuart took a look in a tray containing some of the recent finds. He thought there hadn't been many good things found so far-some pieces of dull brown pottery, a few small rounded things and a rusty bit of metal,-not exactly Indiana Jones stuff.

"What's that?" he wanted to know, pointing at the piece of metal.

"It looks like part of the hilt of a Roman short sword" Rob replied. "You'll be able to recognise it once it's been cleaned up." Despite himself, Stuart was impressed and leaned forward for a closer look.

"Look, these will be beautiful once they've been worked on" said Laura, a pretty auburn haired student. She was holding the small round objects in the palm of her hand. "These are beads, I wonder who wore them?" Under the layers of dirt and soil the beads gleamed dully. Abi stroked them. Immediately she felt a rush, a surge of power which left her shocked and breathless. In her mind, she saw two people, a young man dressed in the uniform of a Roman soldier, and a small, fair haired girl wearing a long, plain tunic with a set of amber beads around her neck. This kind of thing had happened before, when Abi had somehow been touched by the past, a brief, vivid connection which left her shaken and drained.

"Maybe they were given to some local girl by her Roman boyfriend, he might even have brought them from Rome for her!" Laura guessed. "That's what's so amazing about the past, you can use your imagination to make up all kinds of stories!" Abi reluctantly took her fingers away from the beads.

"I see we're missing our baby sitter today!" said Christine with a laugh. The University crowd joined in, but

Abi thought that Rob Dent looked grim, in spite of the laughter.

"Well, I suppose we just have to put up with some things, seeing as our friend Mr. Rivers is putting so much money into our work. Most days we have one of his mates sitting in with us, keeping an eye on how things are going. Maybe Zak wants to check that we don't find anything of value and try to keep it from him. Nice trusting chap!."

Christine hurried to defend Zak. "I don't think it's a case of not trusting us, I think it's just that Zak is so excited about the dig and what we might turn up. You've said that some nights, when everyone is gone, he comes up here and works away by himself. I think he's a frustrated archaeologist!." Rob smiled slightly but didn't answer. The students began stretching and getting ready to begin work again.

Abi had sensed a strain in the atmosphere. Dad was right, she thought, this Zak Rivers does seem to divide the opinion of everybody. They either thought he was great, or they take a real dislike to him. She was glad when Tom suggested moving on. They said their goodbyes and made their way down the hill.

"You know, the more I hear about Zak Rivers the weirder he sounds" Stuart broke the silence. "What's all this about him digging on the hill, when everyone has gone? And why is he watching everything Rob and his students do?."

Tom shrugged. " I agree, it's strange and we should keep an eye on things. Let's forget about Zak now, let's stop by and see Jonty, we're near his place."

They passed through a patch of grass which was called a garden but was full of ancient electrical appliances and bits of old furniture which all looked as if they had been there for several years. Jonty Ginks collected things which he fondly believed would make him a lot of money one day. He dreamed that some day, he would find something of value, something very important, and he would at last make his fortune.

As they knocked on Jonty's kitchen door, Abi noticed a stone box by the wall, looking like any other garden planter, until you saw the skeletons dancing around its sides, all holding scythes and hourglasses, those traditional symbols of death. She recognised it immediately, as the container of Jane Wake's remains which had been discovered last year. Jonty had planted pungent rosemary in it, and Abi was surprised and touched at this sensitive side of the man. She had found that people did surprise you when they did very unexpected things.

"Rosemary for Remembrance" she whispered to herself, her thoughts with the young woman burned to death on Dunchester green.

They were greeted excitedly by Bodger, Jonty's small dog, who was thrilled by their appearance. Jonty himself was pleased to see them. smiling broadly at Abi in welcome. He was watching a football match on TV, and kept the game on, although turning down the volume in their honour. He offered them tea from the large brown pot on the table, but the mugs on the shelf opposite all had a thick layer of stains on their insides, so no one accepted his offer. The conversation was about things in general, with Jonty joining in while still avidly watching the progress of his favourite team. His full attention was gained only when Tom mentioned that they had seen Zak Rivers in the village that morning.

"Zak Rivers!" he burst out, the anger hard in his voice.

"That man's a total…a…a…waste of space!." Tom hid a grin. He guessed that if the girls hadn't been there, Jonty's language would have been much stronger.

"I worked my socks off for him, then he sacks me after two days!"

"What happened?" Stuart asked.

"He got a whole load of lads in the village to do up his big house and the grounds when he first moved in, and it seemed all right,- cash in hand and no travel involved. Seemed ideal. But from the first, we were all treated like prisoners. Had to wear these overalls, blue if you were in the team that worked inside the house, and green if you were out in the grounds. The blues weren't allowed to go outside and the greens had to stay in the gardens. Zak's men were all over, checking up on us, we were watched all the time. I heard from the lads who were in the house that they couldn't even walk around, they had to stay in their groups and work in the places they were put in. Like I said, treated like prisoners, we were." He paused to take a drink from his mug of tea, and looked back at the silent game of football.

"So what happened?" prompted Tom. "Why did you get the sack, Jonty?"

"The second day, we were all called into the dining room to have our lunch and I thought I'd just take a look around, to see what the lads had been doing." Kate and Tom exchanged knowing glances-besides wanting to find out everything about everyone, Jonty Ginks was forever on the lookout to discover that special thing which would make him a rich man. Most likely, he had wanted to investigate to discover if he could "rescue" something of value.

"I looked in the first few rooms and they were empty, all newly decorated and ready for furniture. Then there was the last room along the passage and I sneaked a look in, just for a second 'cos one of Zak's minders had seen me. He came after me and just about dragged me out. Took me straight to the boss man and I was finished on the spot. Sent me the money for the two day's work, and that was it."

"So this last room you looked into- was there anything in there?" Abi asked, eager to keep Jonty's attention on track, as he was now showing great interest in the on screen footballers wearing red and white. Jonty's face creased as he remembered.

"Now that was funny-it was all done out like a laboratory, like you see on telly, benches around the walls, tons of bookshelves and loads of equipment that looked brand new. Don't ask me what all that was for, I just had a few seconds before Zak's heavy pulled me. But that's what I saw- Zak Rivers has built himself a bloomin' laboratory. He's got more money than sense!"

29

Chapter Three

SUNDAY MORNING WITH GRANDAD BILL

Abi knew where she'd find Old Bill that Sunday morning. She'd woken early, just as a light morning mist was starting to lift from the valley. It was now a bright, crisp day, full of the colours and scents of the earth as the year slowly drifted towards its end. She dressed in a jumper and jeans, fed the cats, grabbed an apple and let herself out of the house. There would be time for breakfast later. She found Bill Oaken in his favourite seat outside the old farmhouse overlooking the valley. A pile of newspapers sat on the table in front of him, and his large blue and white mug of tea steamed at his elbow.

Not for Bill the emotion of a hug, just a wide grin and a gesture with his hand that said a lot.

"There you are, Lass! I heard you were back with us. By, it's good to see you, come and sit down!" Abi took the seat opposite him, and they settled into an easy gossip about what had been happening in their lives since the last time they'd seen each other. Nana Hetty had heard her voice, and waved at her through the kitchen window, mouthing the question "Tea?" and Abi smiled and nodded at her. The tea was delivered to her, along with another welcoming hug.

In a pause in the conversation, Abi asked Bill about Zak Rivers. The old man sat back in his chair, thinking about what was in his mind, Bill always measured his words carefully, speaking only after a lot of consideration.

"I don't know" he said at last. "At first, Zak seemed like a breath of fresh air around the place, so full of questions and ideas. He'd read so much about the history of the valley, knew all the old stories and folklore, he was desperate to fit in here. I enjoyed his company, we got on well. Then I noticed that he appeared to know more about the place than he let on. He started asking about the mysteries of the valley, the ley lines and all the strange things that only the old 'uns here know about. You know, everyone grumbles that clocks don't work properly and electrical things don't behave themselves, and that the valley's a strange place in general, but only those whose families have lived here for generations know how special this place really is."

Abi knew that this was very true. Just last year, she had discovered for herself some of the mysterious powers of the earth, when Jane Wake's spirit returned to the valley, seeking justice for an ancient wrong.

Grandad Bill took another long drink from his tea and went on.

"Of course, I told him nothing he shouldn't know, but then I heard that Zak was often in the King's Head, buying drinks for the regulars and pumping them for information. Even hinted that he knew something very odd had happened last summer, and more or less offered a bribe to anyone who would tell him the full story. Now, where had he learned about that? Only the old 'uns knew what really happened, we managed to keep it to ourselves and it never got into the papers. Anyway, all the locals in the pub kept their mouth shut and he got nothing from them. And when he found out that I'd say nothing, he lost interest and stopped coming around."

"We saw Jonty yesterday and he told us about the alterations Zak was making to the Hall" Abi said. "Have you heard he's built a laboratory?" Bill nodded. "What does he need that for?" she wondered aloud. "What sort of experiments is he planning?" They were interrupted by Kate and her brothers, who noisily arrived at that minute, followed by Alfie. Tom went to find Nana Hetty in the quest for bacon sandwiches while Kate and Stuart brought up more chairs to fit around the table.

"Guess who we were talking about?" grinned Abi.

"Man of Mystery-Zak Rivers!" shouted Stuart, blowing a fanfare noise through his fist.

"You know, I'm really bothered about the way he's dividing the village, a lot of people won't hear a bad word about him" Kate said seriously.

Her grandfather nodded in agreement. "Remember he called a meeting of all the local shopkeepers and business people and promised them more visitors to the valley, more trade, more opportunities. He never said exactly what his wonderful ideas were, but everyone was carried away with what he was telling them and thought he was going to do marvellous things for them. Even Paul Rose has been won over, and I thought he'd have more sense. Mind you, I suspect that Zak might have promised him a hefty sum of money to repair the church roof!"

Abi remembered Paul Rose, the young vicar who had played such an important role in giving Jane Wake peace at last. She had not believed that Paul was the sort of person to be bribed in any way, but people often did surprising things. The conversation went on, with Abi hearing more about recent events in Dunchester.

"Paul's even been persuaded to do away with the Winter Light ceremony this year" Kate shook her head at the thought. Tom emerged from the farmhouse carrying a huge tray of crispy bacon sandwiches, his Nan coming behind him with the tea things and he caught Kate's comment.

"Eeh, I used to love that night when I was a kid" he laughed, as if that had all been a hundred years ago. "Going all round the village with my little candle, then jacket spuds and hot soup in the church hall afterwards. Great!" Tom always remembered events through the food he'd eaten then.

Of course, Abi had to know what Winter Light was all about, and Tom nodded to his grandfather to explain, as he himself passed around the tower of sandwiches. Old Bill settled to the telling.

"Christians have always believed that the winter days before we celebrate the birth of Christ are a specially dangerous time, and evil has more power in the world" he began. "Even in the very early times, folk would try to protect themselves against the threat of the darkness. They lit bonfires and made sacrifices to bring back the light and the warmth of the sun at the end of the winter. In the valley, we had our own ceremony, the Winter Light. Church records mention it taking place five hundred years ago, but probably it was happening years before that-centuries before, even. The priest led the people all around the borders of the village, stopping now and then to say prayers and sing hymns.

Everyone carried candles and it was believed we were protecting ourselves from evil, and we'd be kept safe through the dark, cold winter time."

"I always felt safe after that night" Kate confided in a soft voice. "It felt that the whole valley was being tucked up safely and guarded until spring came back."

"Then Zak comes along with his daft ideas, persuades Paul that the ceremony was "a relic of pagan times," he should be more modern in his outlook and put pressure on the parish council to change the ceremony this year. So now we're having some modern do in the church tomorrow night. I'm surprised Paul gave into him so easily about his new fangled ideas, tho' if someone comes along and offers you a few thousand pounds to fix your leaky old roof, you'd want to keep in his good books." Old Bill sat back and drew a deep breath, his anger plain to see.

"Never mind, Grandad, you might be right about a hermit once living on Maiden Hill! Rob thinks there might be some kind of cave there, and they should uncover it soon." Stuart wanted to cheer the old man up, and turn his thoughts to something else. Bill smiled, although obviously still upset and annoyed at what he saw as changes for the worse in the fabric of valley life. Abi joined in, also anxious to encourage her friend to think about more pleasant topics.

"So when was this hermit supposed to live?. And what evidence is there to prove it?" she added cheekily, knowing that Bill, a keen amateur historian, always insisted that any claim about the past had to be backed up with solid, reliable proof. Bill Oaken finally relaxed and smiled at her.

"Well, there's a strong oral tradition-old stories passed on down the centuries, claiming that the Christian religion was brought to the valley by some holy man shortly after the death of Jesus. He was said to have lived on Maiden Hill, spread the story of Christ, looked after the people of the valley and taught them all kinds of useful things.

"You always say to be careful about oral history" Abi reminded him, shaking her head and putting on a stern, teacher-like expression." It must always be supported by facts-remember!" Bill held up his hands in surrender.

"That's right, and so many bad things were happening when the Romans left-the Angles and Saxons from across the North Sea, and the Picts from Scotland were all attacking when the country was left undefended. No wonder we call that time the Dark Ages, so much learning and knowledge was lost. We do have some evidence, mind, we have an account from the very first English historian, Bede himself. Granted, he was writing hundreds of years after, but he tells of a visit he made to the "Hill of the Maidens" as he called it to see where the holy man had once lived. There was no sign of the cave then, it seemed to have been lost in some earth slip, but Bede discovered that local people still remembered the hermit and spoke about him."

Kate was not convinced. "But you did say that Bede was writing years later, and people forget things, they change facts over time. There's no real proof from the time the hermit was supposed to live-what you call 'primary evidence' is there?" Her Grandad paused and looked over the valley.

"Well, I've left the best till last. In the cathedral archives in Durham, there are records from the fort on Crow Hill. Now, as you can imagine, the Romans kept very detailed reports and records, everything had to be counted and listed. So we can see how much grain they had in their storerooms, the equipment handed out to the soldiers, receipts for all the goods bought from local merchants and traders. Even at the very end of their time here, when they knew they'd be leaving, they were meticulous. There's even a mini census, recording all the inhabitants of the valley, along with their jobs and their possessions. The holy man living on Maiden's Dance is there, among all the others. He's even named. He was called Myrddin." Abi looked at him blankly. The strange, soft sound meant nothing to her, but Old Bill wasn't finished. "You might know the Latin version of his name. Merlin."

There was silence among the little group, a silence broken by a yelp from Stuart. "MERLIN!" You mean King Arthur's Merlin? You're having us on, Grandad!"

His grandfather laughed quietly to himself.

"If there really was an Arthur, he wouldn't have been a king, more likely a war chief who fought the invading Saxons, that seems to be what most historians think, but remember we don't really know what was happening at that time. And the dates are all wrong, the "Merlin" on our hill would have lived long before the time of Arthur."

"What kind of holy man do you think he was?" Tom asked. "You said that old stories say he might even have brought the Christian religion."

" Many beliefs seem to have been mixed together then, with people picking out the bits they liked. Maybe he was a druid, they were thought to possess magical powers. They were priests, as well as teachers, judges, historians- it took years to become a druid. Nothing was ever written down and they had to memorise all their learning and skills. Druids were greatly honoured, they were given safe passage wherever they wished to travel, and they could expect a welcome in any lord's feasting hall. They were almost wiped out by the Romans who suspected they were stirring up the tribes against them, but maybe our Merlin convinced the local officer that he was a man of peace."

"So there's no chance of finding King Arthur's body and all his treasure up on Maiden Hill" Tom grinned, feeling a bit let down.

"Sorry to disappoint you, Tom, but no chance at all!" The old man laughed and stretched. Abi decided she should go home and prepare for tomorrow, her first day at her new school. It was important and she wanted to be ready for it!

She paused at the door of the cottage and looked across the valley, yellow and golden in the autumn sunshine. She thought about the ley lines, ancient paths of earth power which some claimed crossed over the countryside, several of them meeting in the village of Dunchester. She liked to think of the lines as faint silver threads, weaving across the valley, making a soft humming noise to themselves.

Chapter Four

~~~~~

"A PLACE LOST FOR CENTURIES!"

Late that Sunday night, Zak Rivers and two of his men drove to Maiden Hill. They left their truck, and taking some necessary tools with them, made their way up to the dig on foot. Zak led the group, lighting their way with a torch, and the gleam from a pale moon helped them to keep to the path. He jumped back as some small creature scuttled in front of him, and he muttered softly. They came to the site and stopped for breath. Zak reached out to stroke the exposed wall of stones in front of them.

"Look, this is either the result of a rock fall, or the locals did it. Question is, did they want to keep people out, or to keep something inside?" he wondered softly. "Rob Dent reckons they'll break through this first thing in the morning. Let's give them a hand!"

They got down to work, and after a few minutes of hard toil, Denny's pick made a different sound against the stones, a hollow and echoing noise. Zak stopped them. "From now on, remove the stones by hand, be very careful, we're nearly there!"

Half an hour later, a hole had been made which was big enough to allow entry into the cave. Zak eagerly pushed the others out of the way. He'd waited a long time for this moment, and meant to enjoy it to the full. Scrambling over the rocks, he raised his torch, letting its beam sweep around the space inside. It was smaller than he'd imagined it, a natural hollow inside the hill, about the height of a man, with smooth walls and a rough floor.

He looked around excitedly, ignoring the other two men as they struggled through the hole in the wall, coughing in air thick with dust from the falling stones.

"Look for anything of value" he told them. "You know the stuff we're looking for. Work as quickly as you can, but don't miss a thing."

Through the thick dusty atmosphere, Zak began to make out signs of habitation. Whoever had once lived there would have known a hard life. There was no hint of any luxury, just basic items, for everyday use. Roughly made mugs and plates were stacked on a large flat rock on the floor. There were traces of a fire at the mouth of the cave, and one or two ledges on the walls had served as shelves, holding more rough pottery objects, along with some glass jars and small bottles. Zak felt a stab of pure wonder as his early love of history touched him again.

"This was so cool! Incredible! Imagine, this place has been lost for centuries" he told himself. He remembered the stories he'd loved as a child, of intrepid explorers finding ancient tombs and temples in the jungle, and he felt the sharp thrill of discovery. Then he thought about the reason for his interest in this place, and the years of seeking and planning which had gone before. He nudged a clay pot with his foot.

"Don't waste time with stuff like this. You know what we're here for."

"Zak! Look at this!" called Denny from somewhere at the back of the cave. He had found a small inner chamber, with an opening so low that Zak had to bend his head to enter. This space was as simple and plain as the first cave, with more ledges on the stone wall carrying bottles, jars and various containers. In front of him was a low, deep shelf which Zak imagined might have formed a sleeping space, perhaps once covered with bracken and animal furs. Now, it contained what looked like the trunk of a tree, roughly worked and shaped. Zak stroked it gently.

"Now what have we here?" he asked himself softly.

"It's not a solid piece of wood, boss" Pete pointed out a seam in the wood, running around the trunk. "I think this is hollow!"

"This is it, lads!" Zak's voice came hoarse with excitement and his mouth felt dry. He remembered that some of the ancient legends described how the great master of magic Merlin had been held captive inside a hollow tree when a rival witch tried to steal his secrets. Could that story have been a garbled account of the thing they had just found? Was it possible they had discovered some secrets from the time of the hermit called Merlin? He felt the familiar thrill as myth and history appeared to flow together, and then he pulled his thoughts back to the present time.

"Right, let's get this down to the truck." He watched carefully as Denny and Pete struggled to lift the heavy mass of the wooden trunk.

"Watch it!" he growled as Pete's foot stumbled over the rough floor of the cavern. The gap they had made between the stones was just large enough to manoeuvre their find through, although it was a struggle, with Zak watching their every move. Then the two men inched their way down the hill to the waiting truck, Zak overseeing their progress all the way, with ill concealed anxiety.

******

Just before Christine began her shower next morning, the phone rang. Abi, idly watching the early morning TV news heard her voice, at first sharp and questioning, then softer and quieter as if she was trying to calm the person on the other end of the line.

"Yes, yes, I'll meet you there in half an hour" she ended the conversation and came into the lounge, shaking her head at what she had heard. David, looking for his keys before setting off to work, glanced at her.

"Who was that?" he asked. "Sounded like trouble."

"It was Rob Dent, absolutely furious, he got a call from Zak early this morning telling him that he and his men had "opened up the cave for him" as he put it. Rob and the others had worked so hard, and had looked forward to that final bit, when they could enter the cave, explore what they had found, and now it won't be the same. He said Zak made it sound like he'd done him some huge favour, but Rob's so mad he's threatening all sorts of things. I wouldn't be surprised if he and the group pack everything in right now and leave. I'd better go now and try to sort it out."

David grinned at her and picked up his keys, "Good luck! I don't envy you!"

Half an hour later, Christine and Rob were standing at

the pile of rocks marking the entrance to the newly discovered cave. Rob had calmed down at the prospect of entering this mysterious place, and Christine tried to improve the situation by joking about Zak Rivers and his need to control everyone and all situations.

"Well, let's see what a mess they've made inside" Rob said grimly and they picked their way over the stones.

Christine shivered as the cold hit her inside the cavern. This must have been a harsh environment, hot in summer and bitterly cold in winter. She turned to look at the view across the valley, with a glimpse of Durham city in the distance. Whoever had lived here obviously wanted peace and solitude, to be far away from the world and its comforts and distractions.

Rob was swinging the beam of his torch over the cave's floor and walls, eagerly taking in everything he could see. He was especially fascinated by the glass containers which he thought may once have held medicines and potions, perhaps made up by the hermit himself. He wondered if it might be possible for the labs in the university to run some tests to discover what they had held, and he mentally added that job to the long list of tasks to be carried out.

Slowly and very carefully, they covered all of the space within the cave, pointing out things of interest to each other, but not touching any of the items scattered around. And then at last they came to the small inner cave. Once again, they looked around excitedly, exchanging ideas. Had this been the bed chamber of the holy man, his private space for sleeping and prayer? Would there be any traces of habitation here? Might there be writings, or other precious artefacts?

"Zak sounded disappointed that he found nothing of great importance or value, but I think this is a real treasure trove" Rob turned to Christine. "It seemed that a hermit really did live here, way back, just as the old stories claimed!" He moved into the smaller space, gazing around, as if looking for something. Christine wondered what was in his mind at that moment, after so much hard work had brought him to this point. Rob gestured around the cave.

"This is what makes everything worth it, Christine! All

the time, the effort, the worries about funding in the department- this is what it's all about, this feeling of being inside a time capsule and you're standing in a place no one else has been for centuries!" Christine found she could hardly speak for excitement, but Rob hadn't finished. "But-I dunno, when you've worked on a lot of sites, you kind of get a feel for them, and there's something not right here. At times you are so close to the people who lived their lives centuries ago, you can almost know them, touch them, but I don't get that feeling here. Zak says he left everything as he found it, but...well, I just wonder..."

Then they were joined by two of the students, and plans were made for the next stage of the work. Lights would be needed here immediately, there had to be a finger tip search of the cave, and every find would have to be photographed, numbered and described, with its exact location marked on a large scale plan of the cave. Seeds found at the bottom of pots would be analysed, to identify the diet of the hermit, and every inch of the site would be studied minutely to see what could be learned. They would run over the time limit originally negotiated with Bill Oaken, but Rob was confident that this would now be extended.

"Abi and the others will be thrilled to see all this" Christine smiled at Rob. "We're going to church tonight for Paul Rose's new service, but I'll ring her and tell her to meet us here straight after school. She and Kate will love to see this, you can almost touch the past here!"

Chapter Five

~~~~~

WINTER LIGHT

Abi enjoyed the first day at her new school. The other people in her tutor group were friendly, and she liked the teachers she met. She found she was familiar with the lessons, and she was even further on than the rest in History and Geography. She did find the day tiring, with so many new things to experience and people to meet, and she was glad to be in the same teaching groups as Kate, with so many new faces and names to remember.

Kate's mother Liz met them both from school and in the car on the way home, Christine rang to tell Abi to change into jeans and warm sweatshirt and then meet her at the site on Maiden Hill. Kate thought she'd like to go along, and soon they were standing at the entrance to the cave, by now made much larger by Rob and his team of students.

The girls entered the cavern, to find the University crew all hard at work, measuring and photographing the site, listing all the items found, and generally becoming familiar with everything in the chamber. There was an air of quiet excitement all around. Lights had been rigged on stands, so that it was easier to see the cave and its contents and Abi felt a thrill at being present at this important time. Kate was drawn to the small inner cavern, while Abi wandered around the main area, looking at some pieces of broken pottery lying in a corner. She was deep in thought, and hardly noticed when the toe of her trainer nudged against something on the floor. Without thinking, she reached down and picked it up-some kind of flat, thin stone, she thought, she'd take it to the lights and examine it properly.

She would never be able to understand or explain her actions later, she had always known that anything discovered at an archaeological site must be left exactly as it was found, but now her mind was a blank, there was no conscious thought, for an instant she had no sense of where she was, or even who she was. She slipped the flat stone into the pocket of her fleece jacket, and forgot all about it.

Abi was fascinated by everything about the dig. She questioned Rob about his finds, and about the life of the hermit who had once lived there. This was her first experience in being in such a place, and she felt awed and excited to think that the last time this cave had known light and voices was shortly after the birth of Jesus. The past was close and real here, and once again she thought about the career she dreamed about-becoming an archaeologist and uncovering the stories of the past.

After tea that evening, Christine and Abi joined the congregation of St. Michael's church for the new Winter Light ceremony. Abi had heard that many people were disappointed that the age-old ritual had been changed, and instead of walking around the borders of the village, a simple service would be held inside the church itself.

"Well!" the older locals had sniffed. "It's earlier than it should be, it's not even 'winter' yet, why everything has been changed!" Still, she noticed, a great many of the villagers had come to this new, though unpopular service.

Everyone began taking their places inside the church, and Abi recognised several familiar faces. She smiled and waved at members of the Oaken family, Hetty and Old Bill were present with Kate and Stuart. There was the vet sitting in the front pew, and Miss Carson who taught in the village school-and the lady who worked in the Spar shop on the main street. Abi's thoughts were interrupted as the organ began to play the introduction to a rousing hymn about following the light. There was a great clearing of throats and several coughs, then the singing began with gusto. The village folk may not be in favour of this new fangled service, but they did enjoy a good tune!

Then Paul Rose took his place in the pulpit. His sermon was about the course of the seasons, the death and rebirth of the earth every year. His voice was thoughtful and gentle, and Abi felt her attention drifting away. She thought about her day at school, and the dim, ancient interior of the hermit's cave, a place which had been lost for so long. She thought about her mother, so far away, and Buster, her cat, being looked after by a neighbour. She became aware that outside, the wind was beginning to rise-it could be a bad night. Strange, it had been such a clear, calm evening as they walked down to the village. Her eyes wandered to the coloured glass window portraying the death of Jane Wake, and one of the first things to attract her to the story of the wise woman when she had come to the valley last year.

The congregation stood, feet shuffling, the organ started up and the choir led the company into another hymn. Abi's attention was dragged back to the present by the sudden vicious howl of the wind, swooping in volume, almost drowning out the music with its shrill, insistent scream. Abi imagined a host of lost souls, frantically trying to get into this place. The singing faltered, as everyone looked around, shocked and afraid by the unearthly noise. Then the strong, true tones of Connie Fletcher took up the melody, strengthening the voices of those around her. The hymn grew in power again, as others joined in, competing with the threat of the gale outside and ending in a triumphant last note. Connie loved singing, especially the old, traditional hymns, and her versions of these often echoed across the village shop, where she dispensed groceries and gossip in equal amounts. Abi thought that Connie- and the rest of the villagers inside the church, would never know how important her part in the service had been that night. The power of the storm had been challenged.

In the pause after the music died, the wind rose again. Abi's gaze was drawn to the front door of the church, where the old fashioned metal latch was moving up and down, as if something was trying to enter.

At first, it was a quiet, cautious movement, as if someone was trying to come into the church without anyone knowing. A few other people had noticed this, and were looking at each other in alarm. Then the door opened slightly, in a huge gust of wind, before slamming shut again. The howling outside increased, as if something alive and desperately hungry was determined to find a way inside.

"Of course" Abi thought. "It can't get in through that door. It'll have to try somewhere else." She didn't want to think what "it" could be. Over the wooden door was a large, plain crucifix, strong protection against evil, and that doorway had seen generations of villagers pass through, come to worship and to focus their thoughts on the God of Light. Surely that entrance would be protected by so many powerful, positive emotions. Abi drew a shuddering breath of relief. The door would hold. It was safe.

Miss Carson now came to the front of the church, prepared to give her reading. In her strong, firm voice, she told how there was a season and a purpose for all things in life. Abi was calmed by the ancient, simple words. She and Christine had chosen seats opposite a small wooden side door hardly ever used. It opened into the oldest part of the graveyard, where aged stones had lost their wording and leaned together as if they were sharing secrets. As Helen Carson paused in her reading, there came a series of enormous bangs against this door. The teacher hesitated only for a second before casting one of her famous "looks" around her, a look which said "you-will-behave-yourself-please" and had subdued children for almost forty years.

The gale rose again, shrill and furious, then the rapping started, angry and insistent against the door. As Abi watched in horror, the solid wood of the door began to bulge slowly inwards, as if under some enormous force.

All she could do was to close her eyes and say over and over to herself "Please make it go away. Let it stop, whatever it is." She felt a chill down her spine as she realised that the door was not secure, and the old heavy bar which was meant to slide across was not in place. Surely the door would smash wide open at any second, and then what horror from the night might enter?

Christine also had realised what was happening. She lunged out of her seat, crossed to the door and swiftly slid the bar into place. The noises outside subsided, although the wind continued to utter low and angry growls. Helen Carson gave Christine an approving nod, and continued her reading in a steady voice.

At last, the service ended, and everyone looked around as they left the church. They all wanted to talk about the storm, which had ended as suddenly as it had begun. Such winds and strange noises! They'd imagined that a lot of damage had been done, leaves stripped from trees, and flowers from a recent burial strewn about, but there was no sign of disorder, just a calm, moonlit night as they returned to their homes.

******

Old Bill Oaken enjoyed smoking a last, forbidden cigarette before he went to bed. That night, he followed his custom, walking around the small orchard, making sure the gate into the yard was secured, then with one of the few cigarettes he allowed himself, he sat on the wooden bench from where he could see the spread of the valley below. He saw the dim lights from secluded homes, and mentally counted off the families who lived there, as he went over the events of that night.

Never in his life had he experienced a storm like that, one of such strength and threat, one which came so suddenly and then retreated as swiftly as it had. And those terrifying thuds on the door-what had been outside the church, trying to come in? He felt a cold fear as he considered that Samhain, the old Celtic festival was approaching. He was always uneasy at that time of the year, for it was said that then the dark powers reached their full strength, and the curtain between our world and the land of the dead was at its most fragile. But always before, the village had carried out its proper protection ritual, the time honoured Winter Light ceremony, which would keep the valley secure over the dangers of the coming season of the dark.

Bill finished his cigarette and made ready to return to the house. Whatever might happen, there was nothing he could do right now, just wait and watch. From the corner of his eye, he sensed a movement, and slowly turned to face the open kitchen door. In the patch of light stood a small, slight man, with a painted face, dressed in animal skins and carrying a spear in his right hand. Bill had seen him before, usually at times when important events occurred in the valley. He had come to think of this figure as the guardian of the place, the spirit of some long dead tribesman-maybe a magician or a shaman, who returned to this magical site at

45

certain times, when he felt the need to make sure all was well there.

Bill put up his hand in greeting, and his visitor raised the wooden spear he carried. Bill wondered if the gesture was one of blessing or warning. The figure vanished, and the old man went into the house, locking the kitchen door behind him. He was thoughtful as he went around, turning off lights before climbing the stairs to bed. It was a long time before he slept, and his dreams were troubled.

Chapter Six

~~~~~~

THE SEASON OF SAMHAIN

In the valley, strange things began to happen, things so small, and occurring so quietly that no one really noticed. Teachers commented that there were more squabbles in the playground, more name calling and bad moods among the children in school. In the King's Head, tempers were lost over games of darts and football matches, and villagers complained that teenagers going to the youth club dropped more litter and their play fights were now starting to worry the elderly folk. Connie noticed that some of her customers were quickly becoming impatient while waiting to be served, or when they were unable to find some item on her shelves. They voiced their feelings loudly, and she became more stressed and upset.

Farm animals seemed unsettled and watchful, and in the village, the dogs sensed something different and strange in the air. Their owners wondered at the snarls and growls from their pets as they met with shadows on their walks. Sudden cold winds raked the streets, and one or two people felt that they were just missing something which was happening in the corner of their vision. There was nothing that could be put into words, but there was a vague feeling that there was something not quite right, some alien presence within the valley.

Then, late one night, Ted Barnwell pushed his way into the bar of the King's Head and asked for a large brandy.

"Brandy is it Ted?" Dan was surprised as he reached for a glass. "That's a change from your usual lager! Everything all right?"

"No, Dan" the farmer shook his head. "I've had a shock, I can tell you."

"What's up?" Dan pushed the drink across the counter to him, and Ted finished it in one large drink. A group of men sitting in the corner stopped their conversation to listen.

"I was driving home from Hexham, my mother hasn't been well lately and I drop in to see her when I can. I came to where the lane branches off to Honeywell farm, you know where I mean?" Dan nodded, he knew the sharp, dangerous bend well. "You have to slow right down there, or else you can end up over the other side of the road," Ted Barnwell continued. "I cut my speed, and that was lucky as suddenly there's this figure in front of me. She was walking on the wrong side of the road-she should have been facing the oncoming traffic, but her back was to me. She was dressed in a long dark coat and an old fashioned hat, like the women wore years ago. And I swear this is true." His voice began to shake. "She turned to me, and she had no face. No face-just an empty space where her face should have been. After I passed her, I stopped and got out of the car. The road was empty, there was no one there."

The group in the corner looked at each other and shifted uneasily. No one was surprised. Most of them had heard of strange happenings lately.

******

Old Mrs. Parker always took the same route when she walked her dog every evening, up by the side of the village hall and then onto the footpath skirting the cricket ground before turning back towards her house. Pip was growing old and lazy and liked frequent stops to smell at any interesting tree or bush, so they made slow progress. On the path ahead, she could see a shadowy figure standing under a dim street light, and blocking her way. She felt a bit uneasy, as far as she could make out, it looked like one of those 'hoody lads' and although she'd never had any dealings with any of them, she was still wary. These youngsters today were so noisy and bad mannered. The papers were full of stories about them.

She slowed her pace, hoping the figure ahead would move on before she reached the lamp, and wondered if maybe she should turn back now. As she approached the still shape, she glanced up, prepared to make some friendly comment about the mildness of the weather. Then she saw the other's face. She took a sharp breath of shock and disbelief. The face of the stranger was moving, pulsating within the hood, and the old lady realised that she was looking at a mass of heaving, seething insects. She recognised flies, worms, maggots, grubs, beetles, amid dozens of other creeping, slithering creatures. She cried out in horror and disgust and turned to run towards the comforting lights and sounds of the village, Pip desperately trying to keep up with his mistress. She heard a high pitched laugh from the figure on the path behind her. Reaching her neighbour's house, she hammered on the door and then fell into the arms of Helen Carson.

******

Jason Freeman was sitting on a bench in his tiny garden facing the village green. He worked shifts in the local frozen food factory and for the next few weeks he was on the middle shift. Many people would find working from four in the afternoon until midnight was demanding. You were going out to work at the time when all your mates were finishing, ready to come home and planning what they were going to do that night, but Jason liked this shift. He simply took the odd hours in his stride. The best time for him, he thought, was coming home in the early hours, the village calm and silent, with only the sound of a distant car to disturb the peace.

Jason always liked to unwind when he got home. He liked to sit outside with a mug of tea or a can of lager, enjoying the coolness of a morning all new and unused by anyone yet. He was doing well, working hard and able to rent his own place, as well as treating himself to a good second hand car. Some of his mates were planning a holiday to France next year, and he had told them to count him in. Yes, life was cool right now. He sighed, yawned and stretched. Time for bed, he thought. Then he saw them.

A troop of Roman soldiers was marching towards him. They came silently, and were surrounded by a faint, luminous glow. Jason was a great fan of historical movies, and these soldiers looked nothing like the tall, handsome soldiers of 'Gladiator' or 'Ben Hur.' Such warriors wore immaculate

49

uniforms and glistening body armour. These men were small, swarthy and looked as if they badly needed a bath and a shave. Above all, they seemed exhausted. Their uniforms were all different, as if various items had been cobbled together to make them usable. The officer, on horseback at the head of the group, also looked worn out, staying on the animal only with a great effort.

Jason couldn't move, he could hardly breathe as the strange company passed him, looking neither left or right. He could hear no sound, no rattle of the harness of the horse, no tramp of a soldier's foot. Then he realised that he couldn't see the lower legs of the soldiers, just their limbs from the knees upwards. He remembered someone had once told him that many of our modern roads follow the path of the original Roman ways, with the ancient roads lying several inches below the surface of today. These men were marching along a road which had ceased to exist centuries earlier. He watched the ghostly troop silently turn at the edge of the village green and then make their way up the hill towards the ruined camp.

"Of course" Jason told himself. "They're coming back from some mission or exercise. They're going back to camp."

******

Ben Irwin lived just across the road from his school, so he never had any excuse for being late. He thought himself to be a big boy now, much too old to be escorted across the road by his mum, who obediently stayed at home at the start and end of the school day, watching him from behind her bedroom curtains.

It was home time, and Lynn Irwin saw the lollipop lady carefully guide her charges to the opposite pavement, and wondered when Ben would appear. Not long now, she hoped, she needed to take him into Durham to buy new shoes. She saw some of his friends cross the road, laughing and chatting as they passed under her window. She glanced at her watch-he must be talking to someone, if he didn't hurry up, it would be dark. The steady stream of children was lessening and Lynn began to feel uneasy. She thought she'd just put on her jacket and wait for him outside, much as Ben would hate this. She grabbed her coat and her purse and walked to the crossing.

She smiled at the lady carrying the large 'STOP' sign

"Hi, Anna- have you seen Ben? He's late!" The woman returned the smile, deposited her latest group of children on the pavement and shook her head.

"No, maybe one of the teachers has kept him behind. He'll be along any minute, I should think." Lynn nodded her thanks and crossed the road. She knew it was very unlikely that Ben would have been delayed by a teacher, as it was school policy not to do this when darkness fell early in the autumn and winter months.

She hurried through the school gates, glancing around the playground-no sign of her son there. Passing along the corridor, she stopped to have a quick look in the hall before making her way to Ben's classroom. His teacher, Mark Walton was at his desk, busy with paper work. A small radio was tuned into a local station, and Mark was humming tunelessly to a popular song. He looked up as she entered and smiled in surprise.

"Mrs. Irwin! Is there anything wrong?"

"It's Ben, he's not come home yet and I thought I'd better come and see what's happened to him."

The teacher looked at his watch.

"Ben left with the others at the usual time. There's no reason for him to stay behind."

Lynn Irwin felt her knees go weak and she slid into a nearby chair.

"Where on earth can he be?" she wondered aloud.

"I'm sure there's no need to worry" Mark reassured her. "Ben's a sensible lad, he's probably got involved with something and forgot about the time, I'll come with you and we'll look for him."

The building was old, and their footsteps echoed as they passed down the main corridor. Lynn remembered her days as a pupil here long ago. Funny how everything seemed so much smaller now, but schools always had the same smell, a mixture of old dinners from the kitchen, floor polish and faint scents of drying macs and fleeces.

51

As they walked, Mark opened doors to look inside various rooms, talking all the time, trying to soothe her worries. Many of the classrooms had big, walk-in cupboards to house books and stationery and Mark didn't forget to investigate these. The library was empty, as were the toilets, wash rooms and the school office. By now, Lynn was feeling cold and sick with anxiety. She began to think it was time to call her husband at work, and then the police, and remembered that she'd left the house without her mobile phone. They halted outside the hall, and it was as if Mark was sharing her thoughts.

"If you wanted to use my mobile to call anyone…" he began, hesitantly, then Lynn turned her head.

"Listen!"

From behind double doors set in the opposite wall, came the sound of a child sobbing.

"That's the gym equipment store" Mark shouted. "Ben! Ben! Is that you?"

He crossed the floor quickly and turned the key which had locked the door from the outside. The small, sorry-looking boy standing in front of them was Ben Irwin. The child's face was marked with tears and his hair stood up as if he'd run his hands through it in his panic. His whole body shook with the force of his sobs and the sight of his mother only made the crying more insistent. His breath came in great hiccupping sobs and he threw himself into Lynn's arms.

"Ben! What were you doing in there? We've looked all over the school for you" she gasped, wanting to laugh and cry at the same time at the sight of his dirty and forlorn face.

"A-a-a-a t-t-teacher put me in there!" Ben finally wailed, rubbing more tears away with a grubby fist. Lynn Irwin couldn't believe what she was hearing.

"A teacher did this? Who on earth would do such a wicked thing?"

She looked at Mark Walton accusingly.

"What teacher was this, Ben?" Mark bent down so that his face was level with the child's. "Who was it?"

By now, the boy was beginning to calm down and he was able to tell them what they wanted to know.

"A different teacher." He sniffed loudly. "He said I was a bad boy and had to be punished. He said his name was Mr. Mercy and I had to stay in the cupboard."

Lynn could feel her worry giving way to fury and indignation. She turned to the teacher beside her.

"I want to make an appointment to see Mrs. Swift" she said coldly. "I don't know who this Mr. Mercy is, but I intend to make an official complaint about him to the Head and the governors. I can't believe a teacher could do this to a child. I want this Mr. Mercy to be disciplined."

Mark looked lost, as if he was desperately trying to make sense out of what was happening. He smiled down at Ben.

"If you go into my desk in the classroom, you'll find some tissues and some paper towels. Why don't you go and clean up, Ben, and we'll see you back here." With one last enormous sniff, Ben hurried off and Mark took Lynn's arm, leading her to a door in the foyer.

"There is no Mr. Mercy, Mrs. Irwin" he quietly explained. "Not now, anyway."

They had entered the staff room, and along the walls there was a display of old photographs, covering many years of the school's history. There was a separate collection of photos of ex Head teachers, all bearing their names and the dates of their headship. Mark pointed to one, close to the door.

"Mr. Mercy" he said.

Lynn thought she'd never known a person to look less like their name. Hair set in a severe parting, cruel eyes glinting behind small, mean spectacles, and narrow, thin lips turned down in a bitter smirk. She could guess how much a child would fear such a teacher.

"Mr. Mercy was Head during the war" Mark's voice broke into her thoughts. "By all accounts, he was an extremely strict, even cruel character. A favourite punishment was to lock children in cupboards, sometimes for hours at a stretch."

Lynn saw that Silas Mercy had been in charge of the school from 1940 until 1946, surely that would make him a very old man by now.

"This man still has something to do with the school?" she wondered aloud.

Mark Walton looked at her for a long time before he spoke.

"Silas Mercy was killed in a bus crash in the 1950's."

Chapter Seven

~~~~~

MISTER MAJICK'S MARVELS

Zak Rivers swirled the last of his drink around his glass and thought he'd better be making his way home. He had a lot to do. The usual group of regulars were sitting in their favourite corner of the bar in the King's Head, and Zak felt from their glances in his direction that they were talking about him. Not that he was bothered about that. He'd been seven or eight years old since the jeering and bullying had last got to him. A slight, geeky lad, Zak hadn't been interested in football or any of the other things boys of his age enjoyed. He was into history, books, and any weird story he could pick up, the stranger the better. Those bumpkins over there! They had no idea…

They had made him welcome in the village at first, impressed by the money he flashed around, accepting his drinks and eager to pass on local gossip, but then he sensed a change in their attitude. Most of these men were of families who had lived in the valley for generations ,and they began to regard him as an outsider, asking too many of the wrong kinds of questions. He smiled bitterly. If they only knew about this place-really knew!. Well, he'd show them all soon. He finished his drink, nodded his thanks to the girl behind the counter and made his way to the door. He opened it just as Bill Oaken was about to enter, and Zak held the door open for him, smiling as they passed. Shame about the old man. Once Zak had thought he could confide in Old Bill, and maybe even include him in his plans, Bill Oaken knew more about the valley than anyone else, his family had farmed there for centuries. Zak shrugged. Like all the rest of the locals, the man was small minded and wrapped up in his own little world.

Dan Rudd began to pour his pint as soon as he saw Bill Oaken enter the bar. He gestured with his head, informing Bill that they should speak in the back room, and his friend

55

nodded. Dan had a word with the girl serving with him and brought Bill's drink along the passage way into an empty room where they could have privacy. Attached to the wall was a glass case, containing a pair of small leather shoes which had belonged to Jane Wake. Both men glanced at the shoes in silent tribute to the adventure they had shared a year ago.

Bill settled in his seat as Dan placed the pint in front of him. The publican wasted no time in voicing his concerns. "Strange things are happening again, Bill" he began. The farmer nodded thoughtfully and sampled his drink, In the village, there were people he knew he could trust-members of families who had lived in Dunchester for year after year. Dan Rudd was one of these, and he served as Bill's eyes and ears in the community. In his job, he learned most things that happened and passed on anything of note to Bill Oaken.

Dan reviewed all the tales he had heard recently-the ghostly appearances, the terrifying events during the Winter Light service, and the growing feelings of fear throughout the valley. Bill listened carefully. He had a story of his own to share.

That morning, Frank Tate had set out to clear a drainage ditch in the upper meadow on Crow Hill Farm. He worked steadily, and completed his task about noon. Gathering his tools together, he placed them in his handcart and thought it was time to take a break. He took a bottle of water from his workbag and enjoyed a long drink, idly leaning against the fence. Funny, he thought, that old scarecrow seemed to be in a different place. Mind, sometimes your eyes could play tricks. The man of straw had stood in the same place for the last two years, quite smart he was, although the weather had got to him and he looked a bit battered now. Young Bill's corded jacket, brown slacks, wide brimmed hat-he'd stood there, hail and shine…Frank's thought abruptly stopped. The scarecrow had moved. At first he thought it was the kids playing tricks, trying to scare him. If it was kids, he'd tell their parents. It wasn't right to spook people like that.

He looked around quickly, to see if there was any sign of the joker. No one was visible. This was a bit nasty, he'd move on now, he didn't want to be there any longer. He bent to pick up the handles of his cart, getting ready to go.

Then he froze in horror as he saw the scarecrow was now leaning against the fence, feet away from where he was standing. One of the creature's legs was draped casually against the other, and its arms were crossed as if it was enjoying a social visit. As Frank gazed, fascinated, the figure slowly turned its head towards him. The blank straw face opened into a hole where a mouth should have been, and there came a rough, hoarse laugh, like the sound of a rusty hinge.

"Hello, Frankie boy!" came the harsh cackle, but Frank had dropped everything, tools, workbag and handcart and was running to beat at the door of the Old Farm House, wanting to spill out his shock and fear to the Boss.

Dan listened to this latest account.

"What do you think might be happening here, Bill?" he wondered.

Grandad Bill put his glass down.

"Seems to me that there's things come into the valley that have no business to be here. We've got ghosts, mischievous spirits, shape changers- but where they come from, and how they got here, your guess is as good as mine. I don't know."

"I blame it all on the fact that we're missing our Winter Light ceremony this year" Dan said forcefully. "You think about it, this is the first time in centuries that it hasn't happened, and we're being bothered by all these weird things. The valley's been kept safe every winter until now. I blame it on Zak Rivers, using his influence to stop Winter Light."

"Maybe you're right, Dan," Bill nodded. "Mind you, all these creatures, whatever they may be, they're mischievous and seem to enjoy scaring folk, but they don't seem out to do any real harm. I'm worried that really dangerous things might come later. If you're right and we have no defences against the dark forces, we're open to even worse things. Don't forget, Samhain's close now, and you know what that means."

Dan leaned forward.

"Bill, this Zak Rivers is dangerous, I'm sure of it. I looked him up on the internet and there's a lot there that we didn't know about him. He's written books and he has some strange ideas. He dabbles in some very unpleasant stuff, and he calls himself a 'magus' and 'master of the dark arts.' Look for yourself and tell me what you think. I wonder what he's planning for the valley? And there's something else. Some of his men often come in for a drink and one of them had a few too many. Told me that Zak talks to a dead man."

******

Bill went home and proceeded to do what his friend suggested- logged onto his computer and looked into the background of Zak Rivers. Half an hour later, he had seen enough. Zak indeed possessed some very weird ideas. He had written several books, all of them investigating the sites he called 'hot spots'-places which he believed showed evidence of the presence of strong earth magic. He argued that in those places, the natural and supernatural worlds came very close, so close that it might be possible to bring the two together. Zak talked about different dimensions and existences, ideas that Bill Oaken couldn't come close to understanding, but he began to see why Zak had wanted to come to Dunchester valley.

He turned the computer off and stared at the empty screen. Zak knew all about the qualities of this area, its ley lines, the problems with electrical and mechanical items, the distinctive personality of the place.

He had chosen the locality carefully. Bill feared that he might be planning some enormous, dangerous experiment- to attempt to contact and let loose dark forces into the valley. Then what? Perhaps Zak planned to turn the valley into some vast theme park. Roll up! Pay your money and see ghosts and all kinds of other nightmare creatures! Good family fun! One more thought lingered in the back of his mind. What was this about Zak Rivers speaking with a dead man? Who –or what could that be? Bill was disturbed and worried as he went downstairs.

******

That night, Tom, Stuart, Kate and Abi were enjoying pizzas and cokes in 'Verona' an Italian trattoria which had recently opened on the village high street. They were celebrating the start of autumn half-term holiday from school, and were looking forward to a week of freedom. They all felt grown up, sharing a meal like this, and Tom was making them laugh, describing how his grandad had recently bought an expensive computer, after years of insisting that these machines would never really catch on.

The door suddenly burst open and a very strange figure capered into the room. It was a clown, garishly dressed in yellow and red stripe pants, a pink spotted jacket and a wide brimmed floppy straw hat with a huge plastic daisy springing from its side. After a second of shocked silence, everyone in the restaurant began to laugh and cheer. Anya, working behind the bar, tried to make herself heard above the din, but her efforts to stop the clown failed, he was determined to make his way among the crowd of diners, smiling and waving to all. Franco, the waiter, went in urgent search for the owner while the clown jauntily danced around, shaking hands with the men and presenting the ladies with flowers he produced from a deep pocket in his pants. On each table, he carefully placed a card, and as he approached Kate, she noticed he wore a badge in his coat, with the words "MISTER MAJICK'S MARVELS" printed in curly, old fashioned script.

Bowing to the friends, the clown solemnly shook hands with Tom and Stuart. Tom grinned widely and nodded at him, but Stuart held back. He had always had a strange fear of clowns, their painted on faces which hid their real feelings, their rough and sometimes cruel humour, their odd clothing. These were pretend people, presenting a cartoon version of their own secret world. The whole idea frightened and disturbed him.

The clown offered the girls two of his flowers, and as he bent towards them, Abi saw that the iris and the pupil of his eyes seemed to blend, into one large dark pool. She had never seen such eyes, and they chilled her, causing her to gasp in surprise. Then Tony, the restaurant owner came bustling from the kitchen, wiping his hands on a towel. He advanced towards the clown, angry that his customers were having their meal interrupted.

"Please! Go! You have no permission to come in here! You are disturbing my customers. Go!" The clown held up his hands in mock surrender, bowing to Tony and offering him a flower. Tony didn't even acknowledge this, but pointed to the door. Wiping an imaginary tear from his eye, the clown went out.

Tom picked up the card from the table. "Come and experience Mister Majick's Marvels on the village green from 20th October" he read aloud. "What do you think that means?"

"We'll soon find out" Stuart answered. October 20th is Saturday- tomorrow!"

Kate looked at her watch and realised that her father was to pick them up for home in five minutes. She hurried them to get ready to leave and went to pay the bill. They left 'Verona' agreeing that they'd had an excellent time.

Young Bill was to meet them in the car park behind the shops, and as they passed a darkened side street, Stuart nudged Tom and nodded at two figures there, deep in conversation. It was Zak Rivers and the clown. Abi looked down at the flower she'd brought with her, and was shocked to see it was dying, fading and rotting even as she looked at it. Soon, there was nothing left but a sour smelling grey dust on her hands.

Chapter Eight

~~~~~

"COME TO THE FAIR"

No one saw them arrive, but by the time dawn broke, an army of lorries and vans had unloaded their cargo onto the village green. A team of workmen clad in green overalls toiled all day, watched by a score of excited children, and by evening, everything was ready. No one could remember a fair being held there before, the biggest village event was the local agricultural show, or the annual village fete. The children watched eagerly as the finishing touches were put to rides and side shows, This was really something special!.

Abi and the others walked down to the village after their evening meal, all pretending that this excitement was so infantile and far beneath them. Stuart sang an old song he dimly recalled from his infant school days... "Come to the fair" he screeched in an off key, high pitched voice. A hard look from Kate shut him up. They were greeted by the hurdy gurdy sort of music you always think of as belonging to a fairground, and even from their mature, very advanced years, they all felt a thrill of excitement as they saw the rows of coloured lights stretched between the trees, and the bright, glowing hues of the attractions spread over the green. Tom had always loved fairs and theme parks, he had visited some good ones, when he'd had the chance. He soon realised that this was very traditional,- old fashioned, even. No computer aided machinery or effects here, just rides and shows that his grandparents would easily recognise.

There was a tent full of slot machines, and little cranes that you had to guide and pick up trinkets within a glass case. Swings that older people called 'shuggy boats' were filled with laughing children and a large roundabout circled, wooden horses brightly painted, their manes flying as they sped on their set path. Shrieks came from passengers on the dodgem cars and younger children played on a huge bouncy castle or hurtled down a steep wooden slide. Above the scene, a banner was strung, showing the grinning face of a clown, and the words 'Mister Majick's Marvels' printed in enormous red letters.

Tempting smells of frying onions, burgers and hot dogs came across the fairground, reminding Tom that, as usual, he was quite hungry. Children and adults wandered around the attractions, drawn by the colours and sounds all around them. Each ride and side show was looked after by a clown, all dressed in a variety of costumes and all wearing Mister Majick badges. Stuart thought their painted faces were menacing, threatening even, their eyes watchful and unblinking, their teeth sharp and yellow under the gaudy lights of the coloured bulbs strung above them.

'Their smiles aren't real' he thought. 'They're fixed to their faces and you don't know what they're really thinking.' He wondered that no one else had voiced these feelings. Maybe no one else had noticed the things he noted. Outside the cocoon of light and noise, shadows lengthened and grew darker at the edges of the village green.

Tom after a lot of deliberation, decided he'd like a hot dog, but Kate sensibly said that they should have a good look around all the amusements before they decided what to do. She stopped to talk to Megan, a girl she knew from school, and when she caught up with the others, she was disgusted to find Tom had bought two hot dogs, and was holding one in each hand. She sighed, always irritated that her brother was one of those annoying people who could eat whatever he wanted and never grew fat or developed spots. 'Porky Pig' she muttered under her breath, spitefully.

They circled the fair doing all the things they wanted-rode on the dodgems, tried to win a teddy bear in a lucky draw, enjoyed the carousel, and sampled the fries from the food wagon. They saw many familiar faces among the crowd, it seemed that most of the village had come to enjoy this treat. Tom noticed two of his friends pass by, and raised his hand in greeting. Poor Darren and Si! They were obviously under strict instructions to look after their little sister! Milly held on grimly to her brothers, trying hard to keep up with them. Tom vaguely noticed that they were heading over to a corner of the fairground, towards some dimly lit attraction that he couldn't make out. Then the three figures were lost amid the crowds.

Kate glanced at the clock in the church tower and reminded them that they still had a few things they wanted to do, and time was going by quickly. The music around them seemed to grow louder, the roundabout circled faster, and the laughter of the excited children was high and shrill. Tom was convinced he would win a prize, and spent three pounds on throwing darts at a target, before realising that he was wasting his money. They were moving away from the main attractions, towards a dark corner of the green. A solitary wooden building stood there, shadowed by a small group of trees surrounding it. Abi thought this place looked lost and sad, few visitors had bothered to come this far, and no wonder. Its paintwork badly needed attention, and a string of dim white lights stretched across its front had several bulbs missing, while those that were still lit flickered fitfully. The words 'Mister Majick's House of Thrills' were painted in faded letters down one side, and a bored looking clown sat inside a payment cabin.

"Wonder what this is?" Tom said. "Let's try it!" Stuart had been examining the building and thought it looked not much bigger than a normal sized house.

"Do you think it will be any good?" he asked doubtfully. "It looks tiny, not worth the money." Abi didn't like the look of the house. It felt threatening, somehow spooky.

"Come on!" urged Tom, digging some money from the pocket of his jeans. "This'll be the last thing we do tonight, we may as well see what it's like, we're here anyway." The clown taking their payment showed no interest in them, and gestured towards the entrance. Tom went in first, pushing open a door which screeched softly. The others crowded in behind him.

Tom's first thought was 'How have they done this?' The outside of the building had given no hint of what lay inside. They were standing in a small hallway, at the beginning of a passage, dimly lit and with what seemed like hundreds of long gauze curtains waving gently in a soft breeze. Tom couldn't see the end of the passageway, and when

63

he looked up, he couldn't make out a ceiling, the billowing curtains disappearing into some mysterious place far above them. Candles flickered on the walls, but they seemed artificial, an illusion.

Were these amazing effects achieved by the clever use of mirrors? By trick projections? Were they generated by a computer? Surely it was impossible to manufacture such things inside this small building, but how could they be faked? A sense of unease began deep in his stomach, and he felt the hairs on the back of his neck standing up. This place wasn't right, it was alien and dangerous.

Behind him, Stuart was pushing forward.

"Whoa!" he whispered softly. "This is well cool!. Look-this place goes on forever, it's awesome! Come on, let's explore!" Tom put his hand out to stop his brother going further.

"Wait Stu! There's something not right here. This place is weird. Can't you feel something's wrong with the air? It's heavy and tastes sour. I can hardly breathe or speak. Let's just go!" The two girls needed no second telling. Both of them had felt strange as soon as they had entered the House of Thrills, and like Tom, they felt a deep sense of unease. Things were very wrong within this place. Abi felt a throbbing headache starting between her eyes, and she was glad to turn towards the door. Only Stuart lingered, wanting to explore further, and Tom had to pull at his sleeve to make him follow them.

They went back into the night, watched by the silent, staring clown in the ticket office, and made their way back towards the main attractions, still in full swing. Tom jumped as a hand touched him on the shoulder. It was Jack Davies, father of Darren, Simon and Milly.

"Tom! I'm glad to see you! I can't find the kids anywhere. I was supposed to give them a lift home twenty minutes ago, but they're nowhere around. Have you seen them?" Tom glanced at the church clock.

"Not for about an hour-and then we never spoke, just waved at each other."

Mr. Davies looked even more worried. "The boys are sensible, but Milly's so young. I can't think what could have happened. I'll have one last look around the fair and then I'll ring the police." His voice sounded strained, and Tom gave him a smile of support. They watched the worried man return into the crowds and Tom turned to the others.

"You know when I saw them, they were heading towards the House of Thrills. I wonder if they went in?" Abi felt a cold shiver down her spine.

"Let's go home" she suggested.

Tom had a frightening dream that night. He was back in the weird House of Thrills, by himself, and he was walking along the dimly lit passage, which stretched in front of him endlessly. His breath was rasping in his dry throat and his heart thudded painfully.His body felt heavy. Every step was a huge effort, yet he felt he must go forward, despite a terror of what he might find at the end of the corridor. He had to push his way through the shadowy gauze curtains, which clung to his hands like the web of some giant spider. He woke up at four in the morning, with his duvet wrapped around his neck. He found it impossible to go back to sleep and finally got up and made himself a cup of tea.

Chapter Nine

~~~~~

"POLICE ARE INVESTIGATING"

It was the leading article on the Sunday morning TV news. Abi heard it as she was bringing a glass of orange juice from the kitchen. The local news reporter, usually chatty and happy go lucky, sounded very serious as he gave an account of the main story.

"Police are investigating the disappearance of three children in County Durham. The group were last seen visiting a fair in the village of Dunchester yesterday evening. We'll bring you more details later in the programme." Although Abi continued listening, she found she was paying no attention to the other items of news. She felt sick when she thought about the missing kids-she knew them all, and little Milly was really just a baby, she'd be so scared and wanting to go home. Abi finished her drink, slipped on her fleece and let herself out of the back door.

She found her friends sitting in the old caravan Tom had taken over and grandly called 'my place.' Abi knew how serious they felt the situation was because Tom made no mention of food or drink. Their faces told her that they had heard the news of the missing youngsters. Their father had rung the parents of the children early that morning, offering to join in any search which might be planned. Abi sensed the others were scared and mystified, and she was relieved when the familiar voice of Old Bill came from the door, asking could he come in. Tom prized his privacy, and entry into his den was by invitation only.

Grandad Bill had brought mugs filled with hot chocolate, and a pile of toasted bread, and Abi felt better immediately. The smell of the drinks and hot buttered toast was comforting, reminder of a safe, normal world, and if Grandad Bill was there as well, everything was sure to work out right!

66

They were soon telling him about their visit to the fair, and their sighting of the missing youngsters.

The old farmer listened carefully, asking questions when he needed more information. He was especially interested in Tom's account of their time in the House of Thrills, and Tom struggled to explain the fear and dread he'd felt there, how things inside had appeared so different to what the outside of the house had hinted at- the actual length of the passage in which they had stood had been impossibly long, and there was no visible ceiling.

"I just wanted to get out, Grandad" he finished. "I felt unwell, and we all thought it wasn't right in there."

"And did you see your friends actually go into this place?" Bill asked.

"Not exactly" Tom said slowly, shaking his head. "I've thought about it over and over, and all I can remember is them walking towards the House, at the edge of the green. I didn't see anything else."

"So many horrible things are happening, Grandad," Kate added. "People are seeing scary things, and now this. Do you think they're all connected?"

Bill Oaken sat back in his chair, his hands behind his head, thinking.

"When you begin to pick out some of the things seen in the valley lately, they're as you say, odd, scary, but not really evil. Yes, some say they've seen ghosts, but except for that little lad who was scared when he was locked in a cupboard, no real harm's been done. Then we have the shape shifters."

Kate put down her mug of chocolate and stared at him.

"What are shape shifters? They sound even worse than ghosts!"

"They're mischievous spirits" Bill continued. "They mainly want to shock people by taking on different, unexpected forms, but they don't want to cause any real harm or damage. They think it's great fun to scare humans- a bit like naughty kids, out to shock. There are tales of them tricking farmers in the old days by appearing as an animal then changing shape completely and running off laughing like mad. Now things seem to be getting worse, very quickly.

We've got three youngsters missing, and that's a completely new development. This 'House of Thrills' sounds horrific!"

Everyone was quiet, thinking of what they'd heard. Tom broke the silence.

"But if we've got these strange things wandering around the valley, where have they come from?" Then his grandfather told them about his recent conversation with Dan Rudd, which had caused him to investigate Zak Rivers. He told them everything he had discovered- Zak's theories about the supernatural, about his belief that there were certain places where the borders between this world and mysterious other worlds are fragile, and able to be destroyed, with the necessary knowledge. Zak called himself a magus, a master of magic, and claimed that he could breach these borders.

There was a stunned silence. Stuart looked troubled.

"Do you really believe all this, Grandad? Do you think it could be possible?"

Old Bill thought for a long time.

"The valley has special qualities, we all know that. We have our ley lines running through the area. Clocks and machinery often behave in strange ways, and any amount of people have stories of unexplained things they've seen and experienced. Just think about last summer and the return of Jane Wake, a woman dead for centuries. There's a strong earth magic here, I reckon, whether you can explain it by magnetism or electricity, I can't tell. Maybe, as Zak thinks, the valley is a place where other worlds touch ours. I think that man may be using his knowledge to somehow 'destabilise' the valley if you like. He's bringing these creatures here for his own purposes. I don't know what he's after, but that's what I think. Zak is playing with us, it's a dangerous game and I don't know how it will end. I fear things will get more serious. According to the gossip in the pub, he's gone off somewhere for a few days,-now does that mean he's planning his next step?"

"It feels like Zak is kind of experimenting with things" Abi couldn't hide her emotions. " He's like a kid with a chemistry set, seeing what would happen if he mixed up all kinds of dangerous things."

"Maybe he wants to set the valley up as a giant theme

park of the supernatural- you pay your money and you meet werewolves and vampires" Stuart suggested, and he couldn't help grinning at the pictures in his head.

"How do you know you can control the 'things' you're messing about with?" Kate wondered. "Surely he's dealing with really dangerous stuff. How can he control it all?"
Tom was trying to work out ideas in his mind before he put them into words.

"What if this is only the beginning?" Bill looked at him sharply. "What if Zak means to buy other places like this, where the earth magic is strong, and it's possible to tap into other worlds or planes or whatever? Just think of the power he could have, if he could call upon supernatural beings or some kind of monsters to appear across the planet? He could hold the whole world to ransom! Is that what he's planning?" They all desperately tried to make sense of these bizarre ideas.

Bill cleared his throat and decided to reveal one last unsettling fact.

"One more thing for you to think about. One of Zak's men had too much to drink one night, and let slip to Dan Rudd that his boss talks to a dead man."

"A dead man?" Stuart was horrified. "This gets worse. What's he doing, and how can we stop him?"

"Steady on, Stupot" his brother calmed him. "Remember, this did come from someone who had been drinking, he may just have got things wrong."

"I think I'd better talk with Paul Rose" Bill decided. "He was once very friendly with Zak when he was promised a lot of money to repair the church. Nothing more has been said about that, and I don't think Paul has such a high opinion of him now. I think we have to plan to perform the old Winter Light service. It might be too late to seal the valley from evil forces, but we can try. We can't forget Samhain is only days away, and we should hold the ceremony before then."

Abi recognised the word. "Samhain,-isn't that the ancient word for our Hallowe'en?" Bill nodded, approving her historical knowledge.

"In a way, but Samhain was much deeper and darker

than our festival. To the Celts, it marked the end of their year and the beginning of the new. It was a dangerous time, when the forces of darkness were about and the spirits of the dead returned to the world of men. Food and wine had to be left on the table for wandering spirits, and you had to be on your guard against their interference."

Tom needed fresh air-he had to try to make sense of all they had heard. He got up to go, and the others did the same. Abi had slipped off her fleecy jacket as she'd sat, and now she pulled it on again. As her hand went inside the pocket, it brushed against something hard- something she'd forgotten about as soon as she'd picked it up in the cave on Maiden Hill. She brought it out and showed it to the rest.

"Look, I picked this up in the cave when I went in with Christine. I know I shouldn't have done that, you have to be very careful not to disturb anything in a dig, and I don't know why I did that.. Something made me pick it up and not say anything. I forgot all about it until now!"

Bill took it from her hand and put on his glasses to see it clearly.

"This is old, Lass" he said at last. The stone was flat, circular shaped, with faint carvings on both sides. "Someone wore this around their neck- see the hole made in the top? And look-I think that's a bull's head carved there, you can make out the horns. On the other side,-that's the shape of a fish."

Stuart was peering at the flat stone. "Why have a bull and a fish round your neck? What do they stand for?"

"The bull was the sign of a follower of Mithras" Bill told him, handing the stone back to Abi. "He was a powerful Roman god, a favourite of the soldiers. He was the god of truth and light. The fish was a very early symbol of Jesus, a secret sign that Christians made, so they could recognise each other."

"So whoever wore this couldn't make up his mind which god to follow, so he wore both signs to keep them all happy! Cool!" Tom grinned.

Bill shook his head. "Maybe it was someone who believed that all roads lead to the same place. If I were you, Abi, I wouldn't worry about how you came to have the stone,

70

you were obviously meant to find it. You never know, it might prove to be important to you some day" He got up to leave with them. "It said on the local radio that the police are holding a meeting for villagers tonight. People are asking a lot of questions about how the police are dealing with these missing young 'uns. You'll probably want to be there yourselves, seeing as you know them."

The friends walked past a field where cattle were grazing contentedly and settled on the wooden bench near the footpath.

"What did you make about all that?" Tom began. "Zak Rivers being some kind of master of magic and bringing all these weird things into the valley. Do you think any of it can be true?"

Kate shrugged. "Well, we do know that unbelievable things can happen here, and lots of valley people are convinced that the place does possess some powerful forces. Christine says it shows 'strong psychic activity.' If we think that's true, whether the cause of that is electrical power or magnetism, or a crack in the earth's crust- or ancient earth magic, as Grandad always claims, then it's only a small step to suppose that you can maybe cross the gap into other worlds or places-or universes-from here."

"Don't forget that Zak came here already knowing a lot about this place" Abi took up her ideas. "He knew what he was looking for. He made himself popular with the villagers, and he was responsible for stopping the old ceremony that's said to protect the valley from evil at this time of the year. He was always planning to let the evil in."

"And we saw him talking to that weird clown that night we went to the restaurant" Stuart interrupted. "Zak seems to have been very busy."

"What about the dead man Zak's supposed to be talking to?" Abi asked.

"Yes" said Tom. "What about that?"

Chapter Ten

~~~~~

DOWN THE RABBIT HOLE

When the friends entered the village hall that evening, it was already full and they were lucky to find four seats together at the back of the room. A table and two chairs had been placed on the stage in front of them, and people were chatting together excitedly. From what she could hear from conversations going on around her, Abi sensed a lot of concern was felt at the way the case of the missing children was being dealt with. Vital hours had been lost before a search was made, and there had been little contact between the police and the family of the youngsters. People were afraid and angry. They had questions, and they needed answers.

A woman came onto the stage and placed two glasses and a jug of water on the table. The audience began to settle, something was going to happen. Then two men entered across the stage. People recognised councillor James Carling, who ushered the second man to a chair. A rustle of discontent spread through the hall. The villagers had expected some high ranking representative of the police to lead the meeting, and to answer their questions. Many had not been pleased by what they saw as lack of action by the authorities, plus rumours of poor communication about the case. Now, here was Will Barber, the local Community Police Officer, a familiar figure around the village, checking on parked cars and tracking down litterers, not really a man to bring calm and confidence in such a worrying time.

Kate turned to Tom. "Why is Will Barber here? I would have thought the police would have put up someone more senior in a case like this."

Tom shrugged. "Maybe it's because the police don't have much to report, they decided to give the job to Will and hope that's OK with people because they know him." Councillor Carling was thanking the villagers for coming to the meeting and then introduced Officer Barber.

Will Barber liked to do things methodically and he had brought some very detailed notes with him. He cleared his throat and began with the arrival of the fair on Dunchester green. The audience began to move in their chairs, becoming restless, they didn't want to hear this, they needed to know how the search for the three young people was progressing. He passed on to give an account of what happened the night before. At last, Colin Davies, uncle of the children, lost patience and stood up from his place in the front row of seats.

"Yes, Will, we all know what happened yesterday and last night, this is just time wasting. What are the police doing today, we certainly haven't seen many of them around the village!" Will became flustered at the interruption, and he was thrown off his stride. He desperately tried to find his place in his report, and to give a positive picture of the investigation.

"All the houses in the village have been searched, and there are interviews going on as we speak. The search is being widened to cover the farms and buildings in the valley. We're tracking down anyone who spoke to the children last night, and descriptions of them have been sent to police forces across the country."

"What about the fair?.That's where they were last seen." Colin's voice came again. "What about those weirdo clowns running it? You never see them without their costumes and painted faces. Real odd bods if you ask me." He sat down to nods and sounds of agreement across the hall and Will Barber struggled to be heard.

"We have searched the fair thoroughly, and the clowns have been very helpful, but they can't tell us anything. The fair will not open again, and the crew will only move on when we are satisfied they can help us no more."

"There were a lot of cars belonging to strangers here last night." A bearded man put up his hand to speak. "The lads and their sister might have been bundled into a car or van and be miles away now."

Will nodded."All the vehicles here last night are being checked through CCTV cameras on the roads leaving the village, but I'm sure you realise this is going to take some time."

"Have police dogs been used to track the youngsters?" Joe Wilson wanted to know. Poor Will Barber looked around, feeling at a loss once again.

"It seems that there would be too many smells for the dogs to pick out individual scents, they'd be confused. The fairground was packed last night."

Low, angry comments were heard among the listeners. Many were not satisfied with the actions of the police and at the slow pace of the investigation. When the councillor rose to thank Officer Barber for his contribution, many people stood, ready to leave. They had learned nothing new and they were worried and afraid, angry at the lack of progress.

Outside, Tom led the way across the main street and towards the fair.

"Tom, where are we going?" Kate asked, fearing his answer.

"I just want to make certain there's no trace of Darren and the others here." Tom sounded grim. Kate sighed- no sense telling him the police must have searched every inch of the fairground, Tom was feeling bad about the disappearance of his friends and their baby sister, he was desperate to get them home somehow.

The fairground was empty and in darkness. A faint gust of wind moved the banner hanging from between the trees and rattled the strings of lights above the attractions. An empty paper bag flapped along the ground and Abi shivered. There was no sign of the clowns, but lights shone through the drawn curtains of the caravans where they lived.

The House of Thrills lay in lonely darkness. Tom wondered what the police had thought when they looked in and saw the mysterious interior- or had the building somehow changed back into a drab, not very exciting side show? And had the House been left open after the investigations?

The front door opened at Tom's touch and although no one wanted to enter, they knew they had to back up Tom, so crowded in behind him.

Abi thought of a drawing from one of her favourite books. Alice was dressed in a blue dress, white socks and black shoes. Her hair was held neatly in place by a band, and she was kneeling, peering down a large hole in the side of a hill. The title of the illustration was 'Down the Rabbit Hole' and Abi wondered what she might find in this particular mysterious place, this 'rabbit hole.'

Nothing in the House had changed. The candles still flickered in their holders on the walls and the long gauze curtains moved slightly and silently. In front of them, the endless passage waited for them. Tom cleared his throat. He hoped he could keep his voice steady.

"Right! Let's go." He led the way. He felt the ground sloping down very slightly under his feet, and the curtains billowed gently around his face, soft as cobwebs. Nobody spoke, they were all concentrating on keeping their feet in the dim light, and wondering what they might see at the end of their journey. On and on they went, now there were no curtains, only bare stone walls, shiny with damp in the faint candle light. Tom's head ached and he found it difficult to breathe. He began to wonder if they would ever reach the end of this passage. They were no longer travelling downwards, the floor was now level and Tom felt the air was colder. Behind him, he heard the others breathing harshly and with difficulty.

Suddenly, it was over. In front of them was a rough opening in the rock, a narrow slit, and then they were outside-if such a place was 'outside.' Looking around, they thought they could never imagine such a scene, not even in a nightmare.

A thick clammy mist surrounded them, making it hard to see the details of tall, looming shapes, tree like, but instead of branches, thick finger like growths reached to the ground. Under their feet, a grey sandy material felt hard and rough, and the air was heavy and smelled of rotting vegetation. Tom was fearful, knowing that the others were looking to him for leadership. Kate glanced down as she felt something touch her foot, and started back in horror as a creature the size of her fist scuttled across her trainer. It was black and slimy, and looked like an enormous slug. She gave a cry and Abi put a hand on her arm to support her.

"What is this place, Tom?" Stuart whispered, and Tom

shook his head.

"I don't know where we are, Stu. We're a long way from home,-I don't think we're even in our own world." Stuart loved watching TV programmes about science, his favourite subject at school. He'd seen documentaries about 'wormholes' which might occur across the universe-portals which could take you into different worlds and times. He didn't really understand how the theory worked, but he agreed with his brother. There surely was no place on earth like this. It felt like a world which was either very young, or extremely old.

Strange rustling, flapping noises came from high up in the tree like growths, as if some winged creatures were moving about above their heads. Stuart worried that they might drop onto their heads and was glad he couldn't see what they were. Tom tried to sound decisive .

"Come on, let's go, the sooner we find the others, the sooner we can get back to Dunchester." Abi had dug her hands into the pockets of her jacket, to keep them warm and also to stop them from shaking in fear. Her fingers touched the flat stone and she drew it out, glad to feel something familiar. She was surprised to see it glowing with a steady, warm light. The carved fish and the bull now stood out clearly on its surface.

Kate was saying she was worried about moving on through this thick fog-what if they lost their way and couldn't find the path back to the tunnel? Abi showed them her stone. "Look, I've never seen it glow like this, but maybe we can use it like a beacon,-something to guide us back ." "That's a great idea, Abi!" Tom sounded relieved. "Grandad did say that the stone might be important to you some time and it looks like he was right. I've never seen a stone do that before, but let's use it!"

He placed the stone high up in one of the tree things and they set off. Abi looked back and was comforted by the steady, reassuring glow, as if something was watching out for them and caring about them. As they walked forward carefully, Stuart looked about him, trying to see through the enveloping, shifting mist. He had the feeling that something was moving with them through the fog, he was glad that he

76

couldn't see what was there, but that also meant there could be all kinds of monstrous creatures following them. They walked on, for what seemed like hours but must have been minutes, their senses strained and then Tom held up his hand. "Listen, I can hear something ahead. Go carefully." The fog muffled any noise, but they could now hear sounds ahead. Then they came to a small clearing, and there, with their sister between them, sat Darren and Simon. Darren had taken off his jacket and draped it over Milly, and the little girl looked tired and very close to tears. They looked up fearfully at their visitors.

"Tom!" cried Darren, "I'm glad to see you. We got lost on the hills in this awful fog and we've been here for about two hours. We didn't want to go further, we thought we'd wait here until the weather clears and then make our way home." The four friends looked at each other. Darren and Si seemed to believe they were lost on the hills above Dunchester village, and that they'd been there for only a short time and not a whole day.

Tom nodded and sat down beside them, speaking gently. "I think we know the way home, Darren, so we'll take you. Here, Milly, I've found some sweets in my pocket, bet you'd like them!" The little girl cheered up immediately and took the sweets. They rose from where they were sitting, Milly thrust her hands into those of her brothers and they all turned towards the distant faint glow of the stone. They reached the place they'd set out from with no more adventures, although Stuart still felt something watching them from the mist. Or was it the tree things examining them? Trees that could see- was that possible? Maybe in this world it was! Maybe plants here could even walk! He'd be so glad to be safely home again. Abi touched him on the shoulder, making him jump.

"Stuart, this is such a horrible place, we can't risk anyone else finding their way here- or any of the awful things from here coming into our own world. My stone seems to be something good, a thing of power. Do you think we can leave it here to guard the entrance?" The boy thought of all the science fiction films and stories he'd enjoyed. They always stressed that travellers in other worlds and dimensions should never leave anything there from their

77

own place, that would interfere with the basic laws of rightness in time and space. Perhaps this object from their own world would somehow check the power of this location. "Yes Abi" he said firmly. "I think your stone belongs here." She reached up and touched the stone, still bravely shining in this grey, frightening world. "Thank you for looking after us" she whispered. "Now you have to stay on and guard this place. Make sure that all the things here stay here!"

The passage way was just the same. Simon mentioned that he was glad the fog had lifted, just as if they were all strolling back to the village. They didn't seem to notice their surroundings- the candles, or the curtains when they reached them. Tom looked at them and tried to work out what had happened to them. The ground slowly rose and then at last they were back in the House of Thrills. Coming outside, Darren took a surprised look at the darkened fairground.

"Well, not much happening here! We'll go straight home and have our supper. I'm starving! See you!" Waving his hand, he escorted Si and Milly off in the direction of their street. The others stared after them.

"Amazing!" Tom said. "They seem to think they've been lost on the hills for a short time-they never mentioned the corridor or the House of Thrills. They've forgotten everything!"

"Let's hope they never remember" Stuart said. Abi thought of the stories she had read years ago, about humans who had found their way into the land of enchanted people who were said to live deep within the hollow hills in their own world. There, they had lived as guests of these lords, hunting, feasting and dancing. On their return to their own homes, they found that instead of days, they had been away for many years and their family and friends were all long dead. Had others, long ago, found one of these lost worlds?

Next morning came the news that the missing youngsters had made their way home after being lost in the hills. They had been examined by a doctor and were fit and well. They were now sleeping peacefully at home.

Chapter Eleven

~~~~~

ZAK TAKES A HOLIDAY

Zak sat outside the London pavement café and enjoyed his very expensive coffee. He checked his briefcase on the chair next to him, constantly patting it as if he had to make sure it was still there. He'd had a very busy few days, visiting museums, private libraries and specialist bookshops, looking for one particular volume. At last, after spending more money than he had planned, he had bought a very special manuscript- the diary of Dr. Dee.

John Dee had served Queen Elizabeth 1st as her scientist and private astrologer. He had claimed to be able to foretell the future, to discover the secrets of nature, and to be able to talk with, and to command spirits. He had written all his experiments in a diary which had been lost for centuries, in fact many believed it no longer existed. Zak Rivers had more patience and more money than most, he had followed several false trails over time, but eventually tracked down the work in a small, back street bookshop. He would never forget the thrill of opening the leather bound diary for the first time and now he was looking forward to examining his treasure carefully when he returned home.

He had spent a fortune, but it had been worth it and now the precious document lay safely in his briefcase. How to speak with and command the spirits! Zak felt a shiver of anticipation and he touched the case with respect once again.

******

Stuart couldn't put out of his mind the thought of Zak speaking with a dead man. Weird pictures played in his imagination until he could think of little else. He had to find out what was happening inside Derwent Hall but he couldn't ask Tom or Kate for help. Tom would take charge of the whole thing, and Kate would immediately tell their parents what he was planning. He knew he could rely on Abi- she was brave and could be trusted in anything. "Abi it is" he muttered and reached for his mobile phone. Zak was still away somewhere and Stuart hoped that security up at the Hall might not be as strict in the absence of the boss.

They started out early the next morning. Abi had not been able to sleep, her imagination filled with dread about what they were going to find. What if they were discovered trying to get into Derwent Hall, and marched back to their parents in disgrace? But Stuart needed her help, he was her friend and she couldn't let him down, and anyway, she knew that he would go ahead without her and she didn't want him doing such a dangerous thing on his own. So, she dressed warmly, shoved a torch into her pocket and quietly let herself out of the house, the cats sleepily raising their heads to watch her as she left through the kitchen door.

Stuart was waiting for her and they set out across the fields in the direction of the Hall. The sky was slowly lightening, and silent cattle watched them curiously as they passed. They reached the boundary wall around the Hall,then walked to a point where the wall gave way to a thick belt of trees. Stuart was hoping there were no alarms or CCTV cameras to detect them as they made their way through the foliage, being as quick but as quiet as they could. They were both pleased to find that they came out of the trees directly opposite a back door of the house. To their relief, the door was unlocked, and they slipped in,-they were inside! Along a corridor came sounds which suggested breakfast was being prepared for the staff. Some one was whistling tunelessly as pans were clashed and cupboard doors slammed.

They crept down the passage, Stuart remembering that Jonty had said the last room contained some kind of lab- surely that would be where Zak was doing these weird things. They passed open doors which showed storerooms and offices with desks and computers, and one which looked like a library. The last door was closed and Stuart cautiously opened it and peered in.

Jonty had been right. This room was a fully equipped laboratory, with benches full of instruments Stuart couldn't recognise, or guess at their function. Only the dim early

80

morning light brightened the room, but above them hung huge scientific lamps which would give enough light for any delicate work to be done. Abi nodded towards a screen in the far corner of the room and they silently crossed the floor. As they edged around the screen, Abi gasped in surprise at the strange figure lying on a narrow bed. The man could have been any age from 40 to 70, his skin paper white, his long dark hair streaked with grey and tied back in a pony tail. His face was gaunt with unhealthy looking smudges beneath the eyes. He was tall and slender, dressed in a hospital gown and various tubes linked him with a bank of machines and monitors at the side of the bed. A grey flecked beard was roughly cut short The man was in a deep sleep, there was no movement, and only the slight, slow motion of his breath told them he was alive and not a carved figure.

Was this the man Zak talked to?- he could easily be mistaken for a dead person, with his stillness, his lack of movement. Stuart gained confidence when it was obvious that there would be no reaction from the figure in the bed. He stared at him, trying to find out all he could from the man's features. At last the boy spoke.

"He is so ugly!" He giggled nervously and used one of Nana Hetty's sayings, "Only a mam could love him."

What happened next shocked and terrified the friends. The man's eyes shot open, and a great roar of rage was heard- but a sound heard only in their brains, where it rolled and echoed like a clap of thunder. Abi put her hands to her head to try and muffle the sound, and Stuart seemed in shock at what had happened, standing open mouthed and petrified. The roar merged into words, with Stuart blasted in a wave of pure fury, heard only within his mind.

"ENOUGH!" came a powerful voice. "Must I be subject to more unworthy treatment and offence? First the man asks me stupid questions and tries to rob my brain, then I have this child, this snivelling worm, this pup, this nithing insult me! I will take no more of this!"

"Is that you talking?" whispered Stuart, staring at the man, eyes open wide.

"Of course it is me, you useless boy. Did the man send you here?" His voice, still heard inside their heads, turned

81

softer and now sounded sly, wary. He turned his head so that he was looking directly at the boy.

"He means Zak, I'm sure of it" Abi whispered. Stuart shook his head and tried to frame a reply in his mind, the way the man was communicating with them. At last, the boy felt he was able to voice words within his head to send his message,

"The man did not send us, we'd get into trouble if he knew we were here". The man in the bed stared hard with his blue unblinking eyes and finally nodded. He looked at Abi.

"Girl, what year is this?"

"This is 2013" Abi sent the thought and he sighed.

"All that time" came the quiet thought. "Too long. Too long."

Abi glanced at her watch "Stu- it's getting late, we should go," She touched the man's arm. Since hearing the date, he seemed deep in his own thoughts, and they needed to know some important facts before they left him. "Who are you?" she asked, trying to make her thoughts sound gentle and polite.

"I am Merlin" came the reply and Abi heard Stuart's gasp. Was this the hermit who had lived in the newly discovered cave on Maiden Hill?

"How did you get here, Mister Merlin?" Abi was desperately trying to be respectful to the bad tempered man in the bed.

"I went to sleep in my cave, I needed to rest and asked my friends to cover the entrance so I wouldn't be disturbed, but I spent too long in sleep. The man found me and he is trying to get inside my brain. So far I have kept him out, but he will find a way into my head and take what is there." He grasped Abi's hand urgently. "The man is evil, if you are not his follower, then you must be on the side of good. You must help me."

"We'll help you" the girl promised, feeling pity for the man, rude as he might be, he was very afraid of Zak Rivers. She wished they could take the hermit to safety that minute. "We have to go now, but we'll come back as soon as we can and we'll bring help. The man's name is Zak, and you're right, he's not on the side of good. Zak is wanting to gain knowledge for his own reasons, you mustn't trust him. We have to go, Mister Merlin, we can't be found here. Zak is away now, so try not to worry, nothing will happen to you until he gets back. Rest and get strong and we'll come back for you" The man stared at her with his very blue eyes, and surprisingly his right eye winked.

******

Abi and Stuart met later to discuss what had happened. It seemed that Merlin had been the hermit of the cave, his body somehow preserved, and taken by Zak Rivers. Zak had discovered from his research that Merlin had lived there, and he had set out to find if anything remained of the wise man. It must have been beyond his wildest dream to find Merlin's actual remains , especially as those remains were intact, and he was well and truly alive, although the man was in a deep sleep.

They knew they had to get Merlin to safety, but they'd need help. They had to tell Tom and Kate, and be prepared for their furious reaction to what they had done.

They set off...... They were not looking forward to the conversation to come.

The brother and sister stared at them in disbelief.

"You did all this yourselves, not telling us?" Tom was annoyed at being left out of it all, but Kate was angry for another reason.

"You actually broke into Derwent Hall! What would have happened if you'd been found there?. The police would have been called and they'd have brought you home in disgrace. Just think what Mam and Dad would have said! You are both pathetic! Abi, I'm surprised at you, I thought you were more sensible than my daft brother!"

"We had to find out who Zak was talking to" Stuart tried to justify himself, to give good reasons for their adventure, he was starting to think they may have gone a bit too far in this thing. "Now we know it was the hermit from the cave, he's alive, and Zak is trying to tap into his mind. We have to rescue him."

Kate looked disgusted, and sat back in her chair, shaking her head

Tom felt himself swept away in the excitement of what he had heard. "So, we get Merlin out of the Hall-then what do we do with him? We'll need a safe place for him." They looked at each other, all thinking the same thing.

******

"No" Jonty Ginks said loudly and firmly. "Most. Definitely. Not. Last year I looked after that Jane Wake and half the time she was here I couldn't think straight, she was messing with my mind and making me do what she wanted. I am not babysitting this wizard or whatever he is. NO"

Tom thought he would have to be very careful about what he said,

"We need to get this Merlin away from Zak, he knows loads of dangerous things Zak needs to find out. If we take him, we'll be doing Zak a bad turn and stopping him getting something he really wants."

Jonty considered this. "And this Merlin man won't get into my head?"

Tom shook his head. "No, Stuart says he's a very gentle and nice person" he looked at his brother, daring him to say something.

Jonty smiled to himself. "I'll get my own back on that Zak Rivers, will I?" Tom nodded firmly. "Right then" Jonty decided "He can come here, but the first time he messes with my mind, he's out on his ear!"

Chapter Twelve

~~~~~

A VISITOR FOR JONTY

They decided to act next morning, with Zak still safely away somewhere, and the staff at the Hall not fully on duty. An ancient wheelchair had been rescued from the garage and a rug placed over the seat. Young Bill's wardrobe had been raided, and a long heavy overcoat borrowed. One of Old Bill's caps and a warm scarf completed the set of clothing and once again, the journey began early in the morning. Tom pushed the wheelchair across the fields, helped by Stuart who lifted it over bumps and hillocks. It was harder going when they reached the belt of thick vegetation and they needed to weave their way carefully through bushes and trees. Stuart worried about how they'd manage pushing the chair with the hermit in it, but decided they'd face that problem when they came to it.

They were relieved to find the back door open again and cautiously they entered the corridor. Abi winced as the chair's wheel scraped against the floor, then jumped as a sudden loud clash came from the kitchen. Stuart pushed open the door to the laboratory and they all edged around the screens to find the man lying there, his eyes wide open. Tom and Kate had been warned what to expect, and they knew the hermit would talk to them in their minds, but it was still a shock to feel Merlin's thoughts creep into their head like probing fingers, wanting to know who they were and if he could trust them.

Tom put a finger to his lips, and remembering what Stuart had said about the man's uncertain temper, he tried his best to make his thoughts respectful. "Mr. Merlin," he began. "We've come to rescue you and take you to safety. You need to trust us, but we have to be as quiet and quick as we can." The man in the bed nodded and gestured that he needed some help to get up. They were surprised to find that, with support, he was able to move quite quickly, but in his long hours alone, Merlin had been moving his limbs in the bed as much as he was able, in preparation for rescue.

Kate held the wheelchair steady, Abi kept watch through a crack in the door, and the boys helped Merlin to the edge of the bed. Tom was annoyed as he realised they had not thought to bring any socks or shoes, but concentrated on getting on the coat and cap, tucking the rug around the man, and winding the scarf high up on his face. In seconds, they had him in the chair, ignoring the sharp, sarcastic mental comments he was making all the time, complaining about his rough treatment. Then they were out in the corridor, trying not to run, expecting to hear a shout for them to stop, then outside and through the trees. It was a bumpy ride for Merlin, avoiding trees, bushes and mole hills, and he protested bitterly and described what he would like to do to the lot of them.

They had an easier time when they crossed the fields and headed for Jonty's house. Merlin watched with sharp, unblinking eyes as Tom knocked on the kitchen door. This was immediately opened by Jonty, who had been warned that Merlin must disappear quickly before his escape was discovered. Once inside, the man looked about him, and again the bitter, biting thoughts came. "What is this place? Where have you brought me? If this is an enchanted place, and you mean me harm, you will live to regret your treachery, you warty toads." Kate thought that for some kind of holy man, Merlin had a bad temper and a nasty tongue.

Tom took one look at Jonty's shocked face and realised they had forgotten to tell him that, like Jane Wake, all contact with Merlin was by thought. Jonty was probably thinking "Not again! Another strange person who will reach me in this awful mind talk and make me do as they want!" He decided to make certain things clear to this man who was looking around his house with such disgust.

"Now look, you, you're only here 'cos I promised my friends I'd look after you, I should think you'd be grateful to be safe, you rude so and so. If you don't behave yourself, I'll tell Zak Rivers you're here!"

"Who is this person?" Merlin asked, looking him up and down scornfully.

"Is he to be my servant?" Jonty looked as if was going to explode and Tom thought that if Merlin had been some sort of a holy man, at times he sounded very arrogant, as if he was used to ordering people about.

"Jonty is our friend, he's helping you but he's not your servant" he said firmly. There was no response from the figure in the wheelchair. "Shake hands, Jonty" Tom nudged him. After a hostile glare, Jonty put out his hand. Merlin obviously had no idea what was expected of him and Jonty nodded to his hand. He put it out gingerly and the two shook hands.

"Now we're mates, see?" Jonty sounded a little more friendly. Merlin stared at him uncertainly. "Don't worry, I can deal with him. First thing, I'll find him something to wear" Jonty said as he showed them out. "We'll all have to lie low, Zak is supposed to be back today so he'll have all his men out looking for him" he gestured with his head. "Just you leave him with me!"

******

They decided to do as Jonty suggested, and keep well away from his house. Once, across the fields, they saw men tramping around, using sticks to search among bushes, before moving on higher up the valley. The searchers didn't seem to be making enquiries at houses- maybe they thought it very unlikely that Merlin would dare to come near to people.

On the second day, Tom had a call from Jonty. "You'd better come here, Tom- and bring your Grandad. Merlin's talking a lot, he's got quite friendly really, he's not a bad old 'un when you get to know him. He's saying all kinds of things, you'd better listen to what he has to say."

This was something Tom had dreaded, now they would have to tell Old Bill everything-how they had broken into Derwent Hall twice, kidnapped someone from there, and the most incredible thing of all, Merlin, the hermit of the cave, was alive and well, and proving to be a very irritable and awkward character. Tom sighed. Well, it had to be done, so the sooner the better.

Bill Oaken found it very difficult to take everything in.

The four youngsters in front of him had told an incredible story, all of them having a lot to say, and each in turn taking up the tale as soon as one stopped for breath. It would be a waste of time telling them what dangerous- and illegal things they had done, it was obvious that they did realise this. He couldn't get his mind around the fact that a man who had lived two thousand years ago was alive and living close by. Bill looked at the friends and his voice was stern.

"You don't need me to tell you that you've done some things that are very wrong, criminal even. This isn't some daft little lark, you could have been hurt, or caught and arrested and you are getting involved in things which are dark and dangerous. Who knows what you might have got yourselves into? You're all growing up, you have to learn to be responsible for your actions and think carefully before you land yourselves in something you can't easily get out of." They were all shamefaced by now, disappointed that they'd let him down and wanting him to trust them again.

Tom nodded. "I'm the oldest Grandad, I should have thought more carefully about what we were getting into. I promise you I'll take a lot more care in the future, and I'll be responsible for the others". The farmer shook his head. He worried about these kids more than they'd ever know, he felt that something evil was approaching, but how could he keep his loved ones safe? He sighed, and got out of his chair.

"Come on, then, let me meet your Mr. Merlin!"

They found Jonty and Merlin watching a football match on TV and Jonty hurried to turn it off. He took great delight in telling them how, when first seeing a programme, the hermit was convinced the figures on the screen were dwarves, or "Little People" imprisoned inside the set, and tried to remove the back from the case to free them. He enjoyed being introduced to the game of football, and because Jonty supported 'the lads in red and white' he joined in, cheering on all teams in these colours, thinking they were all on the same side. He was dressed in a sweatshirt, trainers and jogging bottoms, he'd had a bath and a shave and looked clean and neat. He suddenly seemed younger, and as if he belonged to the Twenty First century. Another big surprise came when he stood up and politely held out his hand to Bill Oaken.

"Hello, you must be Bill Oaken!" His voice sounded harsh and unused, but Abi was delighted. "You can talk properly! Well done!"

Jonty was pleased. "I'm teaching him! He listened to me and copied what I said. Mind, he's still more comfortable talking in that mind language, but we've made a start!" Stuart noticed that Merlin now spoke with a distinct soft north east accent which made him sound like Jonty.

"Mr. Merlin" Abi began. " You wanted to talk with us and you said it was very important. We've brought Grandad Bill with us, we can trust him and he always knows the best thing to do."

"You'd best start at the beginning, and tell us who you are, then" the old farmer encouraged him. Jonty made them all tea, and Stuart noticed he didn't ask Merlin how he wanted his drink, he prepared it as he took his own tea, black, with three large sugars, and the hermit drank it greedily and with enjoyment.

"I was born a prince" Merlin began.

Chapter Thirteen

~~~~~~

MERLIN TELLS HIS STORY

Abi and Kate nodded at each other. So Merlin was of royal blood! That explained his arrogance, and his air of authority, how he talked to people at times. As the man shared his thoughts with them, his listeners were taken away from their places around the kitchen table, and found themselves in a world which existed many centuries ago. If you asked any of them to describe their experiences, they all would have said that it was like watching a giant, 3 dimensional screen inside your mind, complete with sounds, colours and smells, a strange but wonderful feeling.

"I was born in the north country, near the west coast. My father was a king-a minor king, some would say, but he was well respected among his people. I was his third son, my mother had died giving me birth, and I think my father always blamed me for her loss. I was very different to my brothers, and he never seemed to know what to make of me. Gurth and Bran were much older than me, powerful, strong lads who could run and wrestle and our father looked at them with pride."

They watched the small, skinny boy as he wandered through thick green forests, swishing a stick and whistling through his teeth. And here again was the child, curled up in an animal skin in a wooden chair by an open fire making himself small as a cat, watching and listening to everything going on around him. The folk about him spoke freely to each other, and the boy found out all kinds of secrets,-which kitchen girl was pregnant, whose mother was not expected to live until Christmas. Merlin's voice came over the scene…
" I felt I was waiting for something- what it might be, I had no idea but I went on waiting for whatever it was that was coming to me. I felt I was special."

"He sounds a right little prat" breathed Stuart to Tom, and Merlin went on.

"It was the season of Samhain in my sixth year when

90

the stranger came. He asked for shelter in our hall, and of course my father was pleased to agree, for druids had the right to expect a place at any lord's table. His name was Glinn and he was travelling north, to the land of his birth. He looked for shelter as he said there was a great storm due and the snows would come early that year. My father looked at the brilliant blue sky in disbelief, but ordered that a place be set for the visitor at the high table.

Glinn was right, of course, and that night the wind rose and screamed around the hall as we ate, and the snow fell steadily, to be boot high in the morning. The druid stayed with us for the next three weeks, earning his place in the hall by storytelling, by singing, and by performing tricks for his audience. He made an egg appear from the cook's ear and could rekindle a dying fire with a movement of his fingers. He knew my family's history for the last 300 years and could sing about long ago battles and the deeds of heroes whose graves were forgotten. One night, a kitchen lad spilled boiling water onto his foot and screamed in agony. I'd followed Glinn like a puppy, and that night, I saw him take some dried herbs from the bag he always carried on his belt. He added water to make a paste which he spread over the boy's foot, and soon the child's sobs died to a whimper and then stopped as he fell into sleep. I thought this man was wonderful.

In those weeks, Glinn taught me how to write my name, about the healing powers of herbs and flowers, and about the strange people who lived in far off lands. He treated me as an equal and with the same consideration and respect he showed to everyone. He told me of the many gods he'd heard about or read of, he thought all of them showed us there were different roads to reach the same place so there need never be any arguments among their followers. One night I heard him tell my father that he was passing through the north lands talking with the lords to test their views about support they would give in an uprising against the Romans. My father thought that the time for rebellion was gone, although the Empire was weakening, the army still held the country. Rome had given us peace and prosperity, freedom was a lost dream. What would happen if Rome ever left us remained to be seen.

I saw my friend with new eyes-as the ears and heart of our people, a man of influence and power. I knew that I wanted to be like him, I wanted to be a druid. The night before he moved on, I told him my ambition. He warned me of the long, hard training-I would be a man before it was over, and many failed to reach the full grade of druid. Before he left us, he spoke to my father and advised him to take me to the island in the Western sea, where the holy men had their great centre of learning. When Glinn had departed, there came a lull in the bad weather, and father and I set off, wrapped warmly in furs, and with an extra horse carrying sacks of provisions for the brothers.I was now almost seven, and my training must begin soon. We also took money to pay for my lodgings and education over the next years. My father was probably pleased to find a place for me, but when we at last clasped hands and he left me, I saw tears in his eyes, and I was surprised."

The next pictures showed a young man, now easily recognised as Merlin. He walked with other young men and women, all dressed in simple white robes, and they saw him talking, arguing, laughing and studying in a large round open room. Merlin's voice came to them over the scenes... "I cannot tell you about my education, I took an oath that never would I share any of the secrets I learned, and I never have done. Nothing was ever written down, everything we learned by heart from master druids who had learned it all before us. I became skilled in the art of healing and the mending of broken bones. I discovered the ways of men and animals and I memorised the deeds of great heroes and the history of the oldest families in our land. I learned how to speak without words, and I knew the great words of power. The druids were my brothers and sisters and I thought that I might be content to stay there and teach for the rest of my life-and then my feet became ready to walk. I always wanted to know what lay over the next hill.

When it was time for me to leave, I returned home, to find my father had died, and Gurth ruled in his place, supported by Bran. When they understood I wanted nothing from them, my brothers made me welcome, but I felt no ties to hold me there so I accepted some money from them and some food to set me on my way, and I set off in the direction of the rising sun. I used my skills wherever they were needed, I tended wounds and calmed quarrels. I was never turned from any door and when I found myself far from a settlement at the end of the day, I wrapped myself in my cloak and slept under a tree or in some hut in the forest. I met people good and bad, rich and poor and paid for my lodgings with stories and songs and magic, listening and learning all the time.

One day in early spring, I reached a valley in the north east of the country. It was a quiet, hidden place, the grazing was rich and fruit and vegetables flourished, I became fond of the small sweet apples they grew there. I also sensed that this was a place of secrets, where earth magic was strong, and I suspected this was a doorway to places I could not dream about. I stayed there, welcomed by the people for my great learning and my healing power.I made my home in a cave on a hill which had seen many religious ceremonies since the earliest times. There was a Roman camp on the hill above the village, but the soldiers had grown fat and lazy. They didn't bother with me, and I made the valley my home.

But again, my feet longed for the road and I still wanted to know what was over the next hill.I left my valley, always vowing to return. Always I headed in the direction of the rising sun, and decided I would visit a land of secrets and magic I heard of. This was far to the east, a country where the people built huge mountains of stone in which they hid the bodies of their kings. Here, the priests knew high magic, and the secrets of life and death, and I was thirsty to learn the hidden knowledge. I took a ship and came to this land, making my way to the temple and asking to meet the priests. I was treated with respect and kindness, and allowed to join the temple school, but my requests to be taught the deepest secrets went ignored. I had come from across the world, but I was forbidden from learning what I had come for. I waited for my time to arrive-I was good at waiting."

The scenes from Merlin's past now showed him living in a bright, sun lit place, with plain but rich furniture around

93

him. Once again, Merlin was studying and taking part in discussions with other men dressed in simple clothing, but obviously made from fine materials. He was older now, looking almost as he was when they had met him.

"One day, the priests went in procession to the temple to welcome the dawn. There was always a crowd to see this ceremony, as the people believed they would receive blessings from the statues of the gods we carried with us. This was a day like any other, and I watched the faces of people crowding the streets as they bowed low as we passed. I saw a sudden movement in the throng of people as someone pushed their way to the front. A woman screamed and there was a flash of metal as a man launched himself at Apu, the high priest walking in front of the procession.

Without thinking, I leaped at the attacker, even though I was walking three rows behind. I wrestled the man to the ground, grabbing the knife he held, and within seconds, the temple guards were there to pull him roughly to his feet and drag him off to a prison cell. Many willing hands helped me to my feet and brushed the dust of the road off my robes. Apu embraced me, thanking me for his life. The procession went on to the temple and the dawn ceremony went ahead as usual.

After we had breakfast, a servant made his way to me , inviting me to meet with the high priest later that morning. I hoped I would be well rewarded for saving the high priest-maybe I'd receive a gold chain,-holy man I might be, but I enjoyed the fine things in life!

Apu welcomed me, offering me his best wine and some sweet biscuits. He formally thanked me for my quick thinking that morning. It seemed that the would be assassin had a grudge against the priests for raising taxes so much that his shop was in danger of having to close. He looked at me closely and dropped his voice, gesturing me to a chair close to his own.

"Merlin, I have decided to reward you by granting the wish you voiced when you first came to us. No one would even tell you if the rumours were true, that the priests of this land protect the greatest mysteries of life, I must now tell you the truth. We possess secrets so deep that no one would ever imagine what those mysteries might be. We have watched you, and seen your love of learning and your desire for knowledge. Your wish will be granted, and our secrets will be revealed to you. I warn you that the danger is great- you might not survive the ceremony, but if you do, you will possess the deepest, most secret magic that has ever existed.

I breathed deeply. I had no idea that this was to be offered to me, I had no doubt that I wanted this chance, with all my heart. I was told that preparations for my ordeal must begin immediately, I had a lot to learn and must memorise a great many actions and words I needed for the ceremony. Three days before the arranged time, I fasted and prepared myself. Then, the night came, and I was taken to the temple by Apu and two of the senior priests."

The scenes which now played out in Jonty's kitchen were vivid and terrifying. They watched as Merlin and the other priests, carrying flickering torches passed through dark, shadowy pillars and reached a small wooden door hidden away at the back of the temple. One of the priests opened this door and handed Merlin a torch. By its unsteady light, stone stairs could be seen descending into the heart of the temple. Apu nodded to give Merlin courage and he took the first faltering steps. The door closed behind him, and Merlin was left on his own. Down, down he went, taking great care on the narrow steep stairs which looked as old as time. The light from his torch woke shadows to dance around him and then in the distance came the throb of a drum, keeping time with his beating heart. Then came the weird high sound of pipes and the noise of light dancing, stamping feet. Merlin wondered what he would find at the end of his quest.

Merlin looked around and the spell he had woven was broken. "I can say no more, I was sworn to secrecy about that night. It was a night of terror and it changed my life. I stayed with the priests for many more years, my fellow holy men growing old and dying. Apu died and others in their turn took his place. As for me, I never looked different, I never aged. For I had been granted the favour and the curse of eternal life. I would never die."

Chapter Fourteen

"AND I RETURNED TO MY VALLEY"

Stuart looked at his friends seated around Jonty's table. Their faces mirrored his own feelings of shock and wonder. Through the thoughts of Merlin, he had been with him as he descended the stone steps under the Egyptian temple, his torch flickering in the damp, cold air, shadows lengthening on the walls around him. In the distance, he heard the clear notes of a reed pipe and the steady, deep beat of a drum, keeping time with the soft fall of bare feet dancing on the stone floor. With an effort, he returned to his own time.

Bill Oaken cleared his throat and spoke. "Merlin, this is an incredible story. You've learned so much, seen so many things. I want to talk to you about them, but I don't know where to begin."

Jonty Ginks looked totally lost- this man who had been sharing his home claimed to be 2,000 years old! He'd grown close to Merlin and was enjoying teaching him to speak English-with a Geordie lilt and with certain local specialist terms. Why, Merlin was even quickly picking up the rules of football! "Oh no," he thought to himself. "I've only gone and done the thing I did a year ago-taken in someone from the long gone past, but Jane was dead and had come back. At least this Merlin wasn't dead-he's just been asleep for a few centuries." He found himself asking a question of Merlin. "Did you dream when you were asleep?"

As if in response to the friendship Jonty had shown him, the wise man smiled at him and nodded. "There were dreams," came the thought. "Visions and sounds which came from far away. I saw terrible things, acts of cruelty and wickedness but they didn't seem real, just shadows on the walls of my cave."

"Why did you want to go to sleep?" Abi asked. "When

96

did you come back to the valley and the cave on Maiden's Hill?"

Merlin's thoughts came clearly. "The priests in Egypt were very skilled in reading the stars. They discovered that my country was in grave danger. Barbarians were threatening Rome, the mother city of the Empire, the legions were called home and Britain was left defenceless. The Saxons took the opportunity to attack like wolves. My homeland was divided into small kingdoms, and each petty ruler was interested only in his own affairs and unwilling to unite with his brother kings to face the enemy. The land was in danger of going down into the darkness, where the people would remain for centuries, with all the good things we had,-the books, the system of fair laws and justice, the science of building fine towns for the comfort and safety of men- so much would be lost if these hard, warlike men conquered us."

Merlin moved in his chair. "There was a ray of hope written in the heavens. A child had been born and he would become a great war leader. He would hold back the invaders for long enough to keep the light of civilisation alive. This champion of Britain would hold back the dark tide for a generation, -long enough for the invaders themselves to learn some of the ways of the light, so that we need not lose everything. When I heard what was happening in Britain, I knew I must return to my homeland as soon as I could. And so I headed for home, crossing a continent which was being torn apart as the marauding tribes fought over the remaining rags of the Empire of the Romans

I reached Britain, I asked my questions, I searched, and at last I found Artos." At that, Grandad Bill's head raised and he stared at Merlin, but said nothing.

"By that time, Artos was a young man" Merlin took up his story. "He had a Roman father and a British mother. He was a warrior and a dreamer, clever and eager to learn. He was fascinated by the arts of war, and when I told him that I'd studied the strategy of the great Alexander, he questioned me closely, wanting to know how the soldier had planned and carried out his campaigns. Alexander had used horses in his battles, and this cavalry played a decisive role in many of his victories. It was then that Artos had the idea of training horses for war, the Saxons fought on foot and would greatly fear the horse with its power and mobility in battle. Artos was gathering a group of young warriors around him, he called them his "Companions" and they had vowed to follow him to the death.

It was a long period of preparation, but we would not be rushed to strike before we were ready. We planned to have everything in place by next spring, the start of the raiding season for the Saxons. We sent to Gaul for horses, on our side we had young men who were the sons and the grandsons of Roman army veterans and they knew how to train and tend the mounts. In time, we bred our own animals, small and light, but strong and brave as lions. We trained the men who came to us- most of them were farmers, and came armed with whatever they could find that was heavy or sharp. Some even arrived proudly bearing ancient Roman swords or battered shields. We refused nothing and no man. All would be needed in the coming conflict.

When we were ready, we launched an attack on the enemy such as they had never known. The horses proved their worth and we won a great victory. They were good days. Over the next years we crossed the country, chasing the enemy, fighting the invaders wherever they were taking the land and building their settlements. I worked closely with Artos and we became like brothers. I helped him plan his battles, I made sure we had the supplies we needed, I tended the wounded and made sure the dead were buried and remembered in our songs and prayers.

Always we tried to bring the Saxon chiefs over to our side. We made uneasy peace in a dozen different places, Artos constantly promising, persuading leaders of the tribes to keep the treaties they had made. Every day brought fresh questions and new challenges. All places began to look the same to me, until one day we came back to the valley,-this valley. Here we could rest for a while and enjoy a precious time of peace. I loved the fertile farmland, the friendly people, the way the mist touched the hills in the early morning .I still felt that this was a special land, close to the powers and the secrets of the earth. I knew this was the place I'd always been looking for and I made a promise to myself that when all the battles had been fought, I'd return to stay for good.

But the fighting went on and there was always so much to be done-farms burned down by the enemy had to be built up again and restocked, the crumbling remains of the old Roman houses had to be repaired as well as we could manage and the holes in the roads needed to be filled. In our conversations, Artos told me how much he was looking forward to a time of peace, when we could rebuild the towns and schools, and bring fair laws to all the peoples of the land, with Britons and Saxons learning to exist together. This was never to happen. The wars were endless, we held back the invaders in some places, but every year it seemed that they gained more land elsewhere, and there was always a tide of Saxons coming across the seas every raiding season."

Jonty had made fresh tea and refilled all the cups around the table. Merlin took a deep drink and looked far into the distance. He was silent for what seemed a long time, then the thoughts came again. "All the Companions became old, many died in battle or later, because of wounds. I stayed the same, year after year. Then came the final conflict, and Artos was killed. He had been betrayed by a man he thought of as a friend. The remaining Companions went back to the homes they'd not seen for so long, but I had nowhere to go. Then I remembered the valley and I headed north. I was looking for a place of peace, and the people made me welcome. In the time since I'd last been there, the village had grown and now boasted a tavern and more houses.

I fitted into the valley as a hand fits into a glove. I worked hard to help my new friends-I made my home in the cave on Maiden's Dance, I advised the valley people how to care for their animals and crops, I made them medicines and taught the children how to read and write and number. I settled their few disputes and made up stories and songs to tell around the fire on long winter nights. I told them about Jesus the miracle worker, the tales I'd been told on my travels in the East. In return, my friends supplied me with bread, honey, eggs and the small sweet apples they grew. The couple who ran the inn had a son, Jon, a lively lad who came to me one day to tell me he wished to become my servant and to learn from me. He looked after my needs and returned to the village at night. I fell into a routine, easy and peaceful, but then my pride caused me to put all this into danger.

One day a messenger came looking for me. He'd been sent by Collum, a petty king who lived a day's ride north. This Collum loved all things magical and kept a troupe of pet witches and wizards to entertain him with their tricks. The king heard I was now in the area and had sent me a challenge from his people of magic. They wished to meet with me in a series of tests, and the overall winner was to be named the Champion of Magic for all Britain. I was foolish, and took a great pride in accepting such a challenge.

I took Jon with me, hiring a pony for me and a donkey for him and our belongings and we set off for the north. Jon was greatly excited, he'd never ventured so far from his home. He kept asking me questions about everything we saw on our journey. We were received with honour in the hall of the king. Collum was a small, self important man with a red face which spoke to me of bad health and too much wine. As soon as I met his men and women of magic, I knew they were all pretenders and tricksters, possessing no magical skills at all.

The contest which was to last three days lasted one morning, as I showed up their magic to be tricks and clever effects. The king was angry and dismissed them all, for they had lived well at his court and he had trusted in them. We left for home with his thanks and a purse full of silver.

I set a fast pace on the journey home. I had a bad feeling that there was something wrong, and I had to get back to the valley as fast as I could. An hour away, I smelt smoke and the feeling came that I was so familiar with from my battle days, a faster breath, a sickness in my stomach, and the raw dread of what I was going to find.

A Saxon raiding party heading upriver had come across the village, the men had tried to fight them off but it had been a one sided meeting, hardened raiders against farmers. Cattle had been driven off, crops wantonly destroyed, and the wooden homes of the villagers had been fired. Seven men had been killed, including Jon's father. I blamed myself for leaving my friends because of the appeal to my pride. If I'd remained with them, I might have been able to turn away the raiders, using magic or cunning, but I'd left them to their fate without a thought.

I helped them rebuild their homes and take up their simple lives again, but everything was now wrong for me. Life held no pleasure, no hope or future. Not for the first time, I envied those around me who could look forward to ending their days in peace. Not for me. I had to go on forever, seeing so much cruelty and evil in the world. I had never grieved for Artos or for the others I had loved and lost in battles long gone. Now, everything came down around me so that the world felt heavy and life unbearable. I had nightmares each night of death and pain. To me, there was no longer any light or goodness in life."

"Post traumatic stress" muttered Jonty to himself. He was fond of watching TV hospital dramas, and recognised the symptoms from a dozen plots. Merlin had never allowed himself to grieve properly for his battle companions, twice he had lost friends and a community through violence.

"What did you do?" he asked gently. Merlin sighed.

"The priests in Egypt had warned me that throughout my life there would be times when I felt I might not be able to live through them. When that happened, there was a way I could leave my life for a time, I could rest my mind and body, grow strong again. I could withdraw for a space until I recovered and was ready to resume my life and work. I knew which herbs I had to use-I'd brought them with me from Egypt, and I gave my orders to Jon. I had him and his friends hollow out the trunk of a tree, to make sure I would be safe and secure for the time I would be asleep. On a certain day, I would take my drink and leave my life for a time. My friends in the village would then fill in the entrance to my cave and never tell any one where I had gone. They would return there often, to check that I was still asleep and to make sure the cave was still sealed. It all happened as I planned, except for one thing. I had thought to sleep for maybe a year, surely by that time I would have recovered my strength and my readiness for life. But I made a mistake-or maybe it was no mistake, but a secret desire to leave this world for a long, long time. I made my potion, but made it stronger than it was meant to be. So I awoke almost two thousand years after I went to sleep."

No one knew what to say. His was a sad, broken life, so many people he had loved had suffered violence and death. Now Merlin was left, a stranger to this time and the present world, shipwrecked with his memories in an alien existence.

Chapter Fifteen

~~~~~~

SOMETHING EVIL THIS WAY COMES!

Abi was moved by the story she had heard, and she put her hand on Merlin's arm in a gesture of sympathy. You would pass this ordinary looking man in the street and not look at him twice, yet he had led such an unbelievable life. "Artos" Tom whispered. "King Arthur!"

"Cool!" muttered Stuart and she glared at him.

Grandad Bill, sitting on Merlin's other side, placed a friendly hand on his shoulder. "So what happened when you were found by Zak Rivers?" he asked. "Was Zak looking for you? Did he know you would be in the cave?"

Merlin shook his head. Haltingly, and with a lot of thought, he spoke his response. "Zak had done a lot of research about me and the time I lived in the valley. He hoped I might have left writings or items which would have helped him in his search, or maybe my remains would still be there, but to find me in a living state, what he called 'suspended animation' was more than he could have hoped for. He tried to wake me, but I could read his thoughts and I was too strong for him. I refused to be used. I resisted all his attempts and remained safe within myself."

"You said Zak was searching for something, and that you refused to be used" Tom wondered. "What do you mean, Merlin?"

"Zak wants what he has always wanted-knowledge, for if he has knowledge, he possesses power" Merlin answered. "You must understand that there are worlds beyond worlds-strange places we know nothing about, but they exist, side by side with ours. There are certain places on our earth where the barriers between them are thin and if the barriers are broken, these places can act as portals, allowing travel between the worlds."

"And one of these portals is our valley" Kate suggested softly. "So you're telling us that Zak wants to make it possible for people to come into our world from some other place?"

Merlin looked at her for a long moment. When he spoke the soft north country tones he was starting to use were evident. "Not people, Kate…things will come. Zak has been searching for ways he can bring alien creatures here, and control them. He read about the work of Doctor Dee, who became the astrologer and the magician of Queen Elizabeth 1st.John Dee claimed he could speak with creatures from other worlds, and for years Zak has hunted for the diary in which John Dee wrote his secrets, and the words of the highest power which enabled him to make the spirits obey his commands."

"Is that where the strange creatures in the valley have come from-the shape changers and the ghosts and things?" asked Abi. "There's been a lot of frightening things happening lately-but what happens now?"

"Zak Rivers has to be stopped" Old Bill said firmly. "He can't be allowed to go on with this. Can you imagine what will happen if he can bring all kinds of monsters here,- and he can control them? He could end up as master of the world, no government could stand against an army of monsters. There will be much worse creatures than the ones we have seen. Merlin, what can we do?- and will you help us?"

Merlin nodded. "Of course, I agree, and Zak Rivers can't be allowed to carry out his plans. Our world would be wide open to invasion from all sorts of nightmare creatures. It would mean the end of civilization. One thing you must do is to carry out the Winter Light ceremony. The first people to live in the valley were close to the earth and knew how vital it was to set up strong defences here, to keep evil at bay. They created a ceremony which called on the powers of light to protect them in winter, when evil was abroad in the dark of the year. The names of their gods have long been forgotten, but it was always the same struggle- the light against the darkness. The ancient people who first lived in the valley also made a magic to make sure that in every generation, 'Guardians' appear to help protect this place. Usually, these folk don't have any idea of their role, they only know their love for the valley, and are determined to

104

keep it safe. They are always ready to come forward and protect their own place."

Abi thought about the brave group of valley people she had met last year, they had come to help her and her friends bring peace to Jane Wake,-they had offered their help immediately, and without question. Grandad Bill cleared his throat. "The first thing to do is to take Paul Rose into our confidence. We need to plan a new Winter Light ceremony as soon as possible. Zak is obviously going to make his move very soon, my guess is on Samhain, in two days time." He turned to Merlin. "I think you should come, I know you've been lying low here, but Paul needs to meet you and hear what the actual threat is." Merlin was delighted at the idea of an outing. He had seen cars on TV and had longed to sit in one of these 'mighty chariots' as he'd called them in his mind. Jonty was also pleased to be included in the group to visit Paul Rose, and went to find two jackets for Merlin and himself.

******

Ten minutes later, Abi was home. The house was empty and she decided to make herself a cup of tea and sit and think about all that had happened at Jonty's house. She looked out of the lounge window as she sipped her drink and was surprised to see Alfie standing in the drive, staring in at her. She knew that often the dog took it into his mind to wander over the farmland, 'checking out his patch' as Tom described it, smelling any new traces of humans or animals and just making sure that his territory was safe. As she watched, Alfie kept his eyes on her, turning back to the gate. There he sat, looking at her intently and Abi felt certain that the dog was desperately trying to tell her something. Grabbing her jacket, she went to join him and he gave a pleased little noise in his throat which sounded like "at last!"

Without waiting to see if she followed, he led the way to the nearest field, and began to follow the hedge line, smelling the bushes as he went, often retracing his path as if double checking. She followed, wondering what scent was interesting him so much-and also annoying him as he was

105

now uttering low growls and showing his teeth. Abi began to feel uncomfortable, there was something wrong, Alfie could not be clearer with the message. They passed through a gate into the next field, Alfie heading straight for the ancient standing stone which had remained there for centuries.

Head down, nose to the ground, Alfie crossed and recrossed the field while Abi watched. She pulled her jacket closer around her, dark was falling and with it a cold mist was drifting in over the land. Suddenly this place felt hostile and threatening. She'd call Alfie and then they'd head off home. Then, from behind her came a deep rumbling growl, such as she'd never heard before. She wanted to whirl around to face whatever the danger was, but she resisted the urge, and instead, turned very slowly, taking care not to make any sudden move which might disturb whatever might be watching her.

Facing her was the largest, most evil looking dog she could ever have imagined. Its coat was pure black, with no markings or any collar. It stood as tall as her waist, its eyes shining with a weird red glow, its mouth open in a snarl which revealed huge yellow teeth. As she watched, it fell onto the ground into a crouch, and started to crawl towards her, never taking its evil eyes from her face, growling all the time. She was powerless-if she tried to flee, it would catch up with her in a few bounds of its massive back quarters, but if she stayed where she was, she had no chance to fight off such a monstrous animal. She heard another growl close at hand, this time a familiar and reassuring sound, as Alfie approached them, stiff legged and threatening.

Alfie was no longer the family pet, playful and friendly. He was now a growling, menacing creature, fiercely protective of a human he loved. Despite his bravery, Abi knew that there would be no contest between the two- Alfie was strong and powerfully built, and he was fighting to save his friend, but the other animal was some kind of monstrous, feral beast, who would kill or maim without a second thought. She feared for what would happen to both of them when the black dog launched an attack. It continued crawling on his belly towards them, growling softly all the time. Alfie, unafraid, kept on his direct path forward, coming to stand in front of Abi.

106

She was so afraid that she felt she was going to be sick. She dared not take her eyes away from the monster coming ever closer,...and then from the corner of her eyes, she was conscious of a movement. Where it had come from she could not say,-unless it had somehow appeared from inside the standing stone, but a figure now stood alongside her and Alfie, a slight, slim man, dressed in furs and holding a bow and arrow. This was the figure often seen in the fields and by the farm buildings, especially when some momentous event, or time of danger was near. Grandad Bill believed him to be a guardian spirit of the place, coming from a distant past, safeguarding the land and its people. The attention of the black dog had also been captured, and the snarls and growls were now also directed at the man. Slowly and deliberately, the man fitted an arrow to his bow and pointed the weapon at the dog. Before the animal could attack, the arrow sailed across the grass and landed an inch from the animal's nose.

Another arrow was fitted to the bow, but this was not needed. The black dog, as if sensing that he had received a warning and there would be no second given, voiced one last threatening snarl before turning tail and running off into the mist. Abi could only put up her hand in sincere thanks and relief, and the man replied with a similar gesture of his hand. His figure faded gently into the mist and Abi was left staring in wonder. She and Alfie had been saved from a hopeless situation-from a wild beast which looked as if it didn't belong in this world. Her rescuer was a spirit of some ancient inhabitant of the valley, firing an arrow which must have been cut on a day thousands of years ago. She searched the grass in front of her, but there was no trace of the arrow. How could this be? She knew there was no answer to the mystery she had just seen, and she knew she would be forever grateful to the spirit of the ancient hunter.

Kneeling down, she put her arms around Alfie's neck and buried her face in the thick, soft fur. What they had faced today was some evil, alien creature, bent on doing harm. She found it hard to swallow, and her breath came in ragged gasps.

Chapter Sixteen

~~~~~

SAMHAIN APPROACHES

Zak Rivers was furious when he returned to Derwent Hall and discovered his 'guest' Merlin had disappeared. He questioned all his staff, but no one would admit that with the boss away, they had failed to carry out the strict safety measures he always insisted on. They all were certain, no one had heard or seen anything out of the ordinary. Zak sent out his men in teams of two, searching the immediate surroundings. They were to examine sheds, barns and outhouses, to look among trees and undergrowth, they were to cover the remote dales and check every hut and shack. He didn't consider it necessary to ask questions of householders, or to search their property. After all, Merlin couldn't speak or understand modern speech, and he seemed to be half witted anyway so he would never have dared to approach anyone. No, he had hidden himself away somewhere, not too far off, he'd be lying low and suffering from the cold snap now gripping the area. Zak returned to his careful study of John Dee's writings.

In fact, at that moment, Merlin was enjoying his first ever cup of hot chocolate and carefully copying Jonty as he removed the paper wrapping from a Kit Kat. He was discovering he had a very sweet tooth and adored the taste of chocolate.

It was warm and comfortable in Paul Rose's study as the friends discussed the recent events in the valley. Paul had learned a lot after his meeting with Jane Wake last year. He had once thought that usually he knew best about most things, after all he was well educated and held a good degree. His parishioners confided in him and listened to his opinions-but now he knew that there were many things which were simply beyond his understanding.

Paul drank his chocolate and tried not to stare at Merlin.

If this man were to be believed- and the vicar suspected he was telling the truth,- he had lived for over two thousand years and had led the most incredible life. Then there was the bombshell that Zak, Paul's one time friend, was a self styled 'Magus'- a master of magic who planned to bring all kinds of supernatural beings into the valley from other worlds or dimensions or other weird places. The young vicar felt a bit dizzy and shook his head. If this wasn't Dunchester, he'd think he was going mad, but it seems that anything was possible in this valley!

The way Merlin mentioned the word 'magic' so many times, and with an ease which suggested an obvious belief in the subject made Paul Rose feel uncomfortable, but he had become more open minded about all sorts of things recently-magic? Earth powers? Who knows? He was interested in Merlin's claim that in the very distant past, some 'magic' had been cast to ensure that a group of 'guardians' would always be present at times of great danger to the valley. It was hard to believe, but at the same time, Paul could name a number of local people who he would now be contacting to ask for their help in what he was planning to do.

Old Bill had convinced him that the old traditional Winter Light ceremony must be held, as a protection against the coming threat to the valley. Paul now felt guilty in taking notice of Zak's sneers about an 'old fashioned and out of date piece of superstition.' He had given up the old rite too easily- Zak had been plotting all along to gain control of the valley.

It was agreed that Old Bill and Paul would contact the local residents who could be relied on to give their support. Paul would also prepare the prayers and the responses needed in the ceremony, adding extra references to the protection of the village against supernatural enemies. Winter Light would go ahead again in its traditional and ancient manner, and the security of the Valley would be ensured.

******

Zak Rivers was deep in thought. He put down Doctor Dee's book and considered what he had read. John Dee had

109

described the rite he had used to talk with spirits, the words of power and the tasks which must be completed before the ceremony. It was quite clear, and Zak went over in his mind the list of the things he needed. Over the years, he had collected everything, and the book containing the script completed his preparations.

Zak had heard about the sudden decision to hold the Winter Light ceremony. Why should Paul Rose do so at this time, the day before the ancient feast of Samhain? What was so urgent, and what did he fear might happen the next day, to make him take precautions? Zak came to the conclusion that Paul and that meddling old man Bill Oaken may have put two and two together and guessed that he planned to take action tomorrow. And that stupid old fool from the cave had disappeared into thin air, he could expect no help from him. Well, he'd surprise them yet-the Eve of Samhain was a powerful enough time, and they would never expect him to make his move so early! He grabbed a writing pad and began to list the things he would need.

******

Paul had been surprised and relieved by the reaction of the people he'd rang. Old Bill had advised him to stick to a very brief account of the affair and that was the tale he told. The valley was in grave danger, and the Winter Light ceremony was urgently needed to ensure its defence. Very few questions were asked, everyone wanted to know what time they would be needed at the church on the Eve of Samhain, and no one refused to come.

When Abi, her Dad and Christine reached St. Michael's, the rest of the congregation were arriving. Abi had sat down with them and carefully explained everything. Although this was an incredible story, her father and Christine believed it. They had experienced the earth magic present in this place. There was an atmosphere of expectation, and a determination that everyone was going to do the very best they could, no matter what might be asked of them. Abi looked at the faces around her, young and old, and recognised the same calm strength that she had seen when the villagers faced Jane

110

Wake the year before. She had been impressed then at how ordinary people could show such courage when the things they held dear were threatened. Everyone knew of the weird and frightening happenings in the valley lately, and they sensed that this was a time of great peril. Rumour said that Zak Rivers was at the bottom of the trouble. Well, he had no idea what he was up against when he crossed the people of the valley!

The congregation stood as Paul Rose came before the altar. The service would begin with an introduction and prayers, before the whole group went outside, to walk around the ancient boundaries of the village, carrying lanterns and joining in with the old time honoured words which had been printed out for them. At each stop, Paul would place a light, some bread and some water which had been blessed, the ancient symbols of life.

Paul greeted all the friends and neighbours gathered in front of him. He looked at the faces, recognising the readiness he saw there, and the determination to stand together. He quietly explained that the valley was in a time of great danger, threatened by evil forces which must be faced and stopped this very night. Not a sound or a shuffle came from the congregation, everyone watched and listened, unblinking and resolute. Paul paused, perhaps wondering how much more he could say. He wanted his friends to be prepared, yet did not want to fill them with fear. Then, suddenly from a long way beneath them, there came a great hollow booming sound, as if deep within the earth enormous metal doors had been flung open. The earth shook itself, like some great living creature and someone cried out in shock. Everyone looked around fearfully, wondering what might be happening. "An earthquake?" Abi wondered "An earthquake…or something else?"

Sitting further along the pew, she heard Merlin mutter to himself before leaving his seat to stand beside Paul Rose. He said something quiet and rapid to him, and held up his hand as if to calm the feelings of unrest and fright spreading around the church. Abi thought these two men looked like brothers, there was something similar, a certain air about them. Both men were of medium height, they wore their hair

111

tied back and their faces were open and expressive, their eyes light and vivid. "They're both holy men" she told herself. "They're very different, and come from centuries apart, but they are both on the side of the light. I'm sure everything is going to work out well. It must do!"

Merlin spoke in a slow, firm voice, the North East accent noticeable.

"Let us all remain calm, we have a lot to do this night. I believe the noise we have heard is the signal that what is coming to threaten us will come upon the valley tonight, hoping to surprise us before we have fully protected ourselves. We must be ready to face our enemy and I call upon Paul to make a beginning of our fight. I have no idea what we may face, but we must make our stand now, or the valley will never be the same,- in fact, the whole world may be in danger."

Paul bowed his head and led the valley folk in the words of prayers which were centuries old. Beside him, Merlin had closed his eyes and his mouth moved in silent speech. Kate wondered if he was joining Paul in his prayers, or was he repeating words of power even more ancient than the vicar's Christian utterances.

As the prayers ended, and everyone stood up, the feelings of expectation and fear were so strong they seemed to hang in the air like solid things. The vicar and the druid led the way outside, a blast of cold air rushing into the church as the front door was opened. Paul picked up a canvas bag containing the items he would need for the next part of the ceremony. On the stone walls of the porch, ancient weapons had hung for many years, mementoes of long forgotten battles fought centuries ago. Once in a while they were taken down and cleaned by village women who served on a rota to tend the church, but the swords and spears, shields and clubs were dusty and sorry looking, the metal spotted with rust and the half dozen helmets serving as nests for spiders. Dan Rudd signalled to some of his friends, and that was enough for them to quickly take down some of the items and test their weight. Ancient these weapons might be, but surely they were better than nothing!

As everyone came out into the dark, bitterly cold night,

112

a murmur passed from person to person. The church stood behind them, solid and familiar, but this place before them was not Dunchester village. Where was the green, with its neat trees and wooden benches? Where were the lights of houses and shops? Where was the traffic? Where was the King's Head and the restaurant in the High Street? And where on earth was this place?

Chapter Seventeen

~~~~~

OUT OF TIME

This place was not Dunchester, - or not the Dunchester they knew. In front of the church was a clearing, surrounded by a thick growth of trees. A blanket of snow covered the ground and cloaked the rounded huts which could just be made out in the gathering dusk. Smoke rose straight into the air from holes in the roofs, and a skinny dog was scavenging around the settlement. Feelings of fear and disbelief now gave way to a stunned silence, as everyone looked around, some of them checking that the church was still standing there behind them.

Then came Merlin's voice, firm and reassuring. "Don't be concerned, we have come out of our own time and into the past. This is Dunchester as it was, hundreds of years ago. In this way, we can hope that we will be able to do what is needed to be done tonight, and get back to our present time before the dark powers realise what we have accomplished. No one is able to see us, the church will remain as our safe portal back to our own century, but it also remains invisible to anyone living in this time."

"Cool!" breathed Stuart. "How did Merlin manage to do that?"

"I've no idea" whispered Kate. "But I can't wait to be able to get back home. This is what our village looked like long ago, so small, there must be about twenty huts, and they're so tiny. It's incredible seeing this. It seems so much colder here than when we left our time." Tom nodded, he had been thinking the same and hoped there would be hot soup and maybe a jacket potato when they could return. He fastened up the zip in his fleece, shoved his hands deep into his pockets and prepared to move on.

Paul Rose shouldered the canvas bag he had brought, and said he was eager to finish the task so they could return safely and quickly to their present time. Everyone lingered, looking back at a Dunchester that no longer existed, a far off echo of their home. One by one, they turned to follow Paul. Merlin walked beside him, a rock steady presence and support, and the others formed into a tight group coming behind. No one wanted to linger in this strange and unfriendly place. David turned away last. As a scientist, he couldn't believe what was happening. How on earth had this Merlin guy managed to do this impossible, illogical thing?

Paul was beginning to worry about how he was going to identify the limits of Dunchester, in the absence of the familiar sights he knew. Following on past the church, he sensed they were walking along what would become centuries later the road to Durham-but where did the village end? Jonty touched his arm.

"Vicar, I think the border of the village is there, look, there's a spring of water going under the path, just as it goes under the road in our time".He nodded in the direction of a stream bubbling just in front of them. Paul smiled at Jonty. Of course, this was the man who knew every inch of Dunchester, the poacher who always kept his eyes open for something of value' wherever he went.

"Thanks for that, Jonty, I think you're right!" He hurried on, and found a flat stone by the side of the path. Carefully he took out from his shoulder bag a small flask of holy water, and a miniature loaf of bread baked that morning by Mrs. Jackson, his housekeeper, placing them on the stone. He added a small lantern, lighting its candle and then closing the flap to keep it safe. Abi wondered would these things disappear into some other time, or would they be found by the folk who lived in the round huts, and what would they make of these strange objects?

Paul turned and said quietly "The first one." Everyone immediately felt more positive, glad that a good start had been made to their work. As they turned back in the direction of the church, the wind suddenly rose, and snow began to fall, thickly and silently.

"By, the temperature's dropped suddenly" Tom said, raising his voice against the howl of the wind. Abi found that she was feeling colder with every step she took .Soon, she felt the icy wind was finding its way through her jacket and eating into her bones. The snow lashed her face with the force of sharp needles, making it difficult for her to breathe. She felt they were fighting every step of the way against the fury of the storm and around her, she saw the others were all struggling to go on, with every pace an ordeal, but somehow everyone managed to stand against the enemy cold and slowly made progress along the path. Then, as they reached the church at last, the wind died and the snow became little light flurries. The worst seemed to be over, and they all found it a lot easier to move forward.

Jonty took the lead now, and he pointed to a track leading up by the side of the small settlement of huts, in front of them and opposite the church.

"Look, there's where the road heads up to Crow Hill in our time" he pointed to the path. "Up there will be the boundary of the original village, I'm certain of it." They followed him, still feeling the biting cold all around them, but now in good spirits. Tom and Stuart looked at each other, thinking the same thing. Jonty was familiar with all the valley, but how on earth could he recognise a place which would not exist in this world for another thousand years or more?

The ground rose gently away from the huts, and Jonty concentrated hard, looking back and then towards the rise of the land, measuring and calculating in his mind. Finally he halted. "I think this is it" he said excitedly. "This is where Jane Wake's cottage will be, and behind it was the edge of the original village. Paul-this is the place!"

Paul could not be as sure as Jonty seemed to be, but he knew that out of everyone there, it was Jonty's instincts which could be trusted, because of the vast store of local knowledge and geography he had collected over the years. The vicar opened his bag and brought out what he needed. He quickly put the things in place and stepped back. "The second one" he breathed, and a sigh went around the group of friends.

Now they were half way towards the end of their mission and the village was being safeguarded around the four points of its border.

Merlin looked up at the darkening sky and felt that they

must work very quickly to end this business. With the group following Jonty, they passed along a trackway which led around the huts. In their own day, this would be the main street of Dunchester, and Stuart pictured the thriving community the village would become. It must be saved from the gathering forces of darkness. He felt a greater sense of determination, and knew that his friends felt this also. The thin dog they had noticed earlier came out of the shadows and softly growled at them. He may have sensed their presence, or noticed something strange in the wind, but Stuart suspected they had been marked, and felt uncomfortable in the knowledge.

Jonty was leading them towards a band of trees on the outskirts of the settlement. He was silent, his head on one side, as if he was listening to someone, and Kate wondered if maybe he was being helped in his task by something else- some higher power, some agent of the light supporting them in their task that night. Their friend did seem to be acting as if he was making his way with purpose and conviction. He stopped, and gestured to Paul Rose. "Here."

Paul again searched in his bag and found the necessary objects, prepared them and set them down in the shade of a tall oak tree. He raised himself and said quietly "The third one." Abi found she had been holding her breath. This was all going so well- just one more place to identify and protect, then they could return to their own time and know that the village was going to be safe.

They turned back towards the church and the last boundary point of Dunchester. Their steps were faster now, more confident, in a matter of minutes they would be going home, back to their familiar time and place.

It didn't seem to be as cold, the wind had dropped and the snow had stopped. Tom felt almost light hearted, and began to think about his hot supper and how warm his bed would be that night.

A faint high pitched cry caused Merlin to stop in his tracks. On top of the hill overlooking the valley, a host was gathering, and his heart dropped. The forces of the dark had found them, and clearly they were preparing to make sure that the Winter Light ceremony was never completed. The others gasped and murmured together, clustering closer. As they watched, the crowd on the hill was growing as more and more figures joined it. Grandad Bill strained his eyes to make out some of the figures. He realised that he had never expected to see such beings outside illustrations in the pages of old books. The group of friends stood looking on in disbelief and horror.

Chapter Eighteen

~~~~~

THE WILD HUNT RIDES TONIGHT

The scene was lit by great flaming torches set in front of the assembled creatures, their fires blowing in long shining banners. In the forefront of the ranks were dozens of small, ugly figures, all wearing brightly coloured caps, and Bill Oaken believed them to be Redcaps, evil goblins who loved dark and wicked places, keeping their hats bright red by dyeing them in human blood. There was a group of hags, hideously ugly crones, shrieking and waving clubs and sticks. Dwarfs stood firmly together, staring down at them, while nightmarish trolls and trows cavorted before the gathering, in a curious lop sided dance. A troop of clowns stood in the centre of the line, unmoving and still, and a huge black dog sat by them, its great mouth wide and slavering, eyes glowing red in the night. All of the figures were armed with sticks, stones and cudgels and Bill imagined the damage such a host could bring about. At the end of the line, a threatening mass of black forms held their position, their appearance constantly changing, growing and shrinking, the dreaded shape changers. When the attack came, Old Bill knew that these creatures would leech into the minds of the humans and take on the appearance of their greatest fears. Although they normally acted like naughty children, the horrific manifestations they could present would raise fear in the strongest heart.

Merlin could feel the dread and dismay all around him. With just one more stop to make on their journey, it was all over. By the time the friends had gone half way to the church, the attack would come. He made his voice sound calm and full of authority. "I will stay and face them, everyone else should go ahead and make sure Paul completes tonight's rite. I'll hold them back for as long as I can, I still have a few tricks to use". At once, Dan Rudd stepped forward.

"Then I stay with you" he said simply. John's

companions came forward with him, as did David, Tom and the rest of the village men.

"Oh no" Abi whispered to herself. "My Dad!." Merlin sighed.

"You are all foolish, but I can't stop you doing this, you have your free will. We stand together then." While Tom searched for stones and sticks which could be used as weapons, Merlin gave his last instructions to the vicar. They must make their way to the last of the boundary points as quickly as they could, Paul must complete the final task and then they had to get into the church and lock all the doors. He had already laid the magic that would take them back to their own time. The enchanter looked deeply into Paul's eyes, silently speaking his last orders, that once the doors were secured, they must not be opened again, no matter what was heard from outside. He and the men were to be left to their fate. Paul Rose nodded to him, he had understood. Then he turned sharply away.

Kate stared after her brother, he looked taller and older, but still he was so young. Would she ever see him again? She felt tears prickle her eyes and grasped Stuart's sleeve for support.

They were slowed to the pace of the oldest person- Mrs Parker, but no one thought about leaving her, helping her along as much as they could. A great cry went up from the army on the hill, as if an attack would come very soon. Paul looked at Jonty. "I'm going to have a word with Bill and give over command of the group to him, and I want you and I to push forward and place the last items." Jonty nodded, this task must be completed, no matter what the cost was, the valley had to be protected. So, Bill Oaken came to the head of the group while Paul and Jonty hurried forward alone.

Merlin was also certain that the attack would come very soon, the creatures on the hill seemed to be gathering their strength and spirits. He grasped the tall wooden staff he had found when they circled the village and desperately tried to think of a plan. Since awakening from his long sleep, he had been aware that his powers had weakened, his wits were not as quick as they had once been. Could he summon up the power to bring down a protective mist upon his friends?- or somehow enchant the small stream running at the bottom of the valley to become a raging river?

Paul and Jonty reached the corner of St. Michael's with the sound of loud cheering and mocking heard plainly from the hill. Then a drum started up, a slow insistent beat, and they looked at each other in despair.

"Quick, Paul- the old border point will be up past the side of the church-you need to get your things together." Paul had frozen to the spot. It was bitterly cold again, but worse than the cold was the black despair he now felt growing inside him. It was as if he had been robbed of all the joy and gladness he possessed, leaving only a sense of hopelessness. There was no laughter, no light, no faith inside him, and he felt he could not go on. The path they had to follow was filled with threatening shadows, the young vicar felt an overwhelming sense of emptiness and horror. Jonty seemed to somehow sense his despair, for he grabbed Paul's bag and pushed on into the darkness.

"Paul, the dark is inside your head, you have to fight it!"

At the touch of his friend's hand, the black spell was lifted, and the two men together opened the bag and prepared the articles inside it. Paul's deep breath was heartfelt as the job was completed."We did it,Jonty" he whispered. Then the beat of the drum took on a quicker, more urgent rhythm.

"They're still coming" Jonty said hoarsely."They're going to test us!"

The clowns started to hurry down the hill, in time with the beat of the drum but the small group in the valley stood firm. In the glow of the torches, the fangs of the clowns showed yellow, their eyes unblinking. Closer they came, and behind them, the rest of the figures of nightmare joined the charge as the drum took up a faster, more threatening sound.

Now the whole massed line of creatures was advancing down the hill and into the valley, Merlin desperately hoped that the last position had been protected- but how secure was the defence offered by this ancient rite in the face of so much dark magic?

As the mass of clowns neared, whooping and shouting, there suddenly came a sweet, haunting blast from a horn, causing the attackers to stop in their tracks. "What is it, Merlin?" Tom asked softly, the dread strong in his tone. "What's coming now?". Merlin drew himself up to his full height, and in a voice full of wonder and relief he answered softly "It's the Hunt! The Wild Hunt! They're here!."

Standing behind him, Dan Rudd murmured "The Hunt rides tonight, then. They have a prey for the first time in centuries!"

There now came the high yelps from excited dogs, growing closer by the second and Tom felt the panic rise in his throat. He wet his dry lips and tried to keep his voice steady, but he was aware that it sounded weak and scared. "Are these more creatures of the dark?"

"The Wild Hunt belongs neither to the dark or the light" Dan told him. " The Hunt serves to protect the Old Laws, which lie outside darkness and light. The Laws were set out at the beginning of Time and must never be challenged. Tonight the very fabric of our world and of other worlds has been defied, and matters must now be righted." Tom shivered. The sounds of hounds in full chase was now almost upon them, but the cries came from above his head, among the low dark clouds which brooded over them. The others had stopped in their hurried progress to St. Michael's and were staring back at what was happening.

Finally, Tom dared ask the question which had been in his mind. "And who leads the Hunt?" His words were little more than a whisper. Merlin's look seemed to come from a thousand miles away.

"Herne the Hunter, Father Odin, the horned god. He had been called many names in different times, but he is always the same and never changes."

The clouds parted, through the gap poured a pack of maybe twenty hounds- great lurcher dogs with shaggy black fur and yellow, shining eyes. Their mouths were open wide in full cry, and their calls became terrible shrieks as they hurtled to earth and caught sight of their prey. Among the dogs rode a troop of hunters, mounted on pure white horses, prancing and dancing proudly as they carried the riders. All the chasers wore helmets elaborately fashioned in the shape of animal heads- boar, lion, stag-and their armour gleamed in the torch light. At the head of the company, a knight sat astride a huge warhorse, obviously the leader of the Hunt. His head was covered with a helmet, but he was now too far away for Tom to notice the details.

Back up the hill were chased the creatures of the dark, screaming in anger as they went, and as the valley people watched, a huge crack appeared on the hillside. Within seconds, the army of monsters disappeared into the earth, their cries and screams echoing behind them. With a hollow grating sound, the crack came together, leaving no trace of what it had taken and disposed of. Silence now came to the valley, as the huntsmen gathered their hounds together and quietened them. The whole band now gently came to stand before Merlin and his friends.

Now, they could see that the leader of the Hunt was wearing a helmet cunningly shaped in the face of an owl, the feathers of its wise, ancient features each formed from pure gold. The eyes behind the helm were a curious yellow colour, strangely flecked, sharp and alert. As he approached them, the man took off his face covering, to reveal a young –old face, calm and fair. Light hair fell to his shoulders, and his whole appearance was regal and serene. Merlin fell to his knees and took the hand the stranger offered him.

"Artos! My Lord!"

"We meet again, Merlin, as I told you we would. You still look the same, my friend, your magic must still be powerful. And you are still fighting for your valley?"

"Some things in life are well worth fighting for, Lord. You yourself taught me that-and I have some loyal friends here who have stood by me-here is one of them, this is Tom Oaken." Merlin brought Tom forward and the boy was stunned. All his life he had loved stories about King Arthur, England's hero king. He knew about Arthur's knights and their deeds- and even if the stories weren't true, they had still thrilled him. But here was Arthur himself- or was he Herne…Odin? He remembered his manners and bowed low to the man on the white horse. Arthur leaned down to him and took his hand.

"Keep the valley safe" he said softly. "You, and the other Guardians."

"Tom nodded, "I will….My Lord" he replied. Arthur donned his helmet again, saluted all the valley folk, and wheeled his horse round towards the direction from where they had come. The whole company moved off, the hounds now silent, their red mouths open and panting. Slowly, the company disappeared from sight, leaving the valley folk staring after them.

"I have just met King Arthur!" Tom whispered to himself. "King Arthur!" No one said anything as they moved to rejoin the rest of their friends near the church. They all felt a sense of great wonder and awe, and could not begin to understand the events of this night. As they met, the groups merged, the spell of silence was broken as friend greeted friend and hugged and laughed. They could now go home!

******

When they came back to Dunchester, it was a clear and cold evening. It felt they had been in that other time for many hours, but their absence had lasted little over an hour of their own time. A hot supper had been prepared in the church hall for all of them, and Tom felt that the food was the best he'd ever tasted. The meal became a celebration. Although they could never tell their story to other people, the group knew that they had faced enormous dangers that night, and in doing so, they had safeguarded their beloved valley.

During the next hours, all of the furniture and equipment was stripped out of Derwent Hall and taken to some other place. Zak Rivers was never seen again, but as he had been investigating other "hot zones" where paranormal activity was strong, it was suspected he had encamped to one of these sites. As Stuart remarked, "The further away from us the better." Dunchester was allowed to sink into its tranquil and ordinary daily life. For the moment. But then, the valley was always so peaceful and calm, it always had been, and always would be……..

124